The Sea's Embrace

The Sea's Embrace

Angela Steed

Black Lyon Publishing, LLC

THE SEA'S EMBRACE
Copyright © 2008 by ANGELA SMEAL

Our books may be ordered through your local bookstore or by visiting the publisher:

www.BlackLyonPublishing.com

Black Lyon Publishing, LLC
PO Box 567
Baker City, OR 97814

ISBN-10:   1-934912-09-3
ISBN-13:   978-1-934912-09-6
Library of Congress Control Number: 2008935748

Written, published and printed in
the United States of America.

Black Lyon Paranormal Romance

To Dad, my hero.
May you find your Atlantis is paradise.
I love you always.

Chapter One

A white lily slowly floated toward her as she sat on the concrete wall, touching the surface of the small pond with her fingers. Watching the young goldfish swim quickly away from the ripples she made, she smiled.

The warm breeze lightly played in her long dark hair as the soft curls danced at the small of her back. She let out a deep sigh, trying to relax. Her lavender satin skirt waved slightly at her ankles, caressing her pale skin lovingly as she rested her chin on her knuckles and her elbows on her knees.

Being in such a position was an awarding sensation, or so Katherine Shaw thought. The press considered her an architectural mastermind, a brilliant artist as she captured the essence of an ancient artifact in her latest masterpiece, which wasn't quite finished.

She strived to learn everything she could, and felt she'd surpassed the blueprints of architectural structures, happily moving on to her hobby. Having a profound fascination for archaeology, she'd sold everything she owned back in the States, dropped her entire workload at the architectural firm, and moved to England.

It was like a backwards episode of "The Beverly Hillbillies" as she moved from her five-bedroom mansion off Lake Michigan to a small, rather run-down apartment in London. She loved it, though the few mice living with her were a bit of a nuisance.

It was a small sacrifice for living her life the way she wanted. Since college she'd worked only to provide herself with a comfortable life. But now she worked for her own ambition, enjoying the luxuries of her job at the London Museum of Art and Archaeology.

As she posed for the camera under the first arch she'd sculpted for the museum, she desperately wanted them to wait until it was fully constructed. Insecure of her work, she'd let them talk her into being photographed for *National Geographic* magazine before it was done.

"Thank you, Miss Shaw," the over-zealous man behind the camera said, extending his hand out to her. "You're quite photogenic."

"Thank you, Don." She happily acknowledged his compliment and took his hand. He shook it lightly and then helped her to her feet.

She straightened her skirt with her hands, wiping the small pebbles of dirt from her backside. And with a short turn, she faced the arched structure.

"When do you think it'll be finished?" he asked curiously, glancing at the dug up dirt the excavator had made a few days ago. Katherine had refrained from looking at the mess, but his wayward glance made her eyes turn. She pursed her lips for a moment, wishing again she hadn't let him photograph the piece until it was done.

"I'm just waiting on them to finish digging so we can lay the concrete foundation for my next arch. They'll need to dig two more holes on the other side for the center pieces, and then lay the cobblestone floor. I imagine it'll be another few weeks."

"I can see how disturbed you are about it," Don said in a reassuring voice. "Don't worry, I'll be back to photograph when it's complete. The article won't run until we get a finished photo."

Happy to hear it, she grinned at the short photographer, but he wasn't looking at her. His eyes were fixed on the green, coffin-like box.

"I still can't believe it," he said, quite fascinated by it. "The museum curator told me it broke the heavy steel cable when they lifted it out of the water."

Katherine nodded. "I was there when it happened. I thought the boat was going to sink from its weight. It was as if it didn't want to be removed from its resting place." She gazed at the artifact, running her eyes over its extraordinary designs.

"An enchantment," Don chimed in. "Some people are labeling it as an evil presence, if you can imagine."

"I know," she replied. "Protestors stand outside the museum everyday wanting us to take it back where we found it."

"It'll blow over." He tossed his camera over his shoulder and gave her an abundant grin. "It was very nice to meet you, Katherine. I'll see you soon."

"Thanks, Don. It was a pleasure."

She lied, partly. It was definitely a pleasure to meet the short young man, but there was no doubt the photographs were premature. If only the workers hadn't stopped digging. She wished she knew how to operate their heavy machinery so she could finish it herself, but only after changing out of her heeled shoes.

She pulled them off her feet and hopped up onto the cement wall. With her arms crossed behind her back, she began walking, watching the box as it sat ominously on an altar in the center of her newly constructed fish pond.

Strange indeed, she thought. The museum deemed it a solid block of metal, but for some reason she sensed it was hollow. There had to be something inside, something incredible, and possibly far more ancient than they thought.

Ever since they'd found it in a shadowy cove in the depths of the English Channel, she'd had vivid dreams. They were so real she could almost feel the beautiful white horse beneath her as they galloped through golden fields.

She'd seen herself dressed in a white flowing gown, walking up the stone steps of a temple, awaiting someone to step forward and offer her a blessing. But she always awoke after catching a glimpse of dark hair.

The vision left her as she dropped down from the wall and into the soft excavated earth. Her bare foot hit something solid, and she fell to her backside cursing under her breath from the pain.

She raised her foot, inspecting her stubbed toe for a moment, and then turned her attention on what had caused it. Careful not to stub her fingers on whatever it was, she flattened her hand and gently shoveled soft clumps of soil until she'd dug a small hole.

She struggled to find anything. No rocks, no sticks, only soft soil rich enough to grow a beautiful garden in. But when she dug further, she caught her finger on something smooth and solid, and grabbed hold of it.

She pulled it out of the dark pit and inspected it. A rock, the size of a softball and just as round, lay beautifully in her dirty hands. Except for a few coarse pieces missing and a small crack down the center, it was perfect.

Tiny fragments sparkled in the sun as if someone had sprinkled it with silver glitter. And oddly enough, it carried a very faint glow.

"Katherine?" A familiar voice startled her from her unusual find. "What are you doing playing in the dirt, dear?"

She stood up, palming the ball in one hand and turned to face Ty Benson, the quite handsome archaeologist she'd known since she came to the museum a year ago. He wore his usual half-grin on his pale pretty-boy face, watching her intently. His thick blond wavy hair caressed his shoulders as he folded his arms over his chest, obviously finding humor in her childish desire to dig in the dirt.

She returned his smile as she carefully stepped back onto the cobblestone walkway beside him. She tossed her shoes to the ground and slipped them on her dirty feet.

"I hit my foot on something when I jumped into the dirt," she said, holding up the ball to show him. "And this is what I found."

Ty briefly glanced at the unusual rock that oddly quit glowing, and then returned his gaze to her. A tint of pink showed in his high-boned cheeks, showing he was more interested in her rather than what she'd found.

"Are we still on for tonight?" he asked, completely enthralled with her big blue eyes. "I hope we can find a little romance this evening."

She smiled as he palmed her arm. She sincerely hoped he wasn't interested in commitment, because she surely wasn't, at least not with him. Unfortunately, he'd made it clear he was terribly into wooing her.

He'd planned an evening picnic at the park, a bottle of wine to keep them warm under the beautiful fall leaves, and a blanket in case it became too cool during the horse and carriage ride he'd proposed. It sounded fantastic, but way too romantic for the friendship she preferred with him.

As he walked her to the museum door, he touched her back. He talked a mile a minute, telling her what was on the dinner menu in detail. Although she could hear what he was saying, she wasn't listening.

A sudden sense of urgency hit her and Ty's voice faded completely. Her heart quickened its pace, and a strangling sensation worked into her throat as if she were drowning. Her skin tingled as if she'd sat too long and sleep had set in the parts of her body that hadn't moved. And within the numb sensation came a pain so excruciating she felt tears come to her eyes.

Agonized by torturous throbbing, she screamed, begging for someone to help her, but it wasn't the sound of her voice crying out. This voice was deep and malevolent.

"Are you all right, Kat?" Ty's voice brought her back to her senses. The pain dissipated as she felt his strong hands gently shake her back to reality, and her disoriented glance came about to his concerned face.

She walked behind her desk and sat down in her chair, fumbling the ball in her hand as she tried to figure out what had just happened.

"I'm okay," she replied, unable to take her eyes off the sparkling orb.

"You left me for a moment," he continued, sitting down on the edge of her desk, slumping slightly with his arms dangling between his legs.

"I did?" she asked curiously, and then agreed intriguingly. "I did."

"Where did you go?"

"I'm not sure," she answered, returning her gaze to his.

She set the ball down on her desk and smiled. As if a sudden weight was lifted from her shoulders, she returned to her normal composure.

"Listen, I'm going to head home and get ready. I suggest you do the same for I'll be picking you up in two hours."

Katherine stood up, giving him a nod as he left, but deep down she was screaming at him. He had a terrible power-trip attitude, mostly due to his wealth. His proper British accent and fine-tuned body were two reasons she didn't want to get involved—too charming and cocky. There was no doubt she thought him to be very handsome, but there was nothing there for her.

He took her on excursions, including the one with the infamous metal coffin sitting on the altar outside her window. He showed her the markings surrounding the entire thing and told her it was thousands of years old, possibly linking back to the time of the Druids.

He feared cracking it open to see the interior would remove its worth to the world, or possibly the extra wealth he was receiving with the rise in ticket sales to the museum. Money was always a matter of importance, especially when it came to his discoveries, and the museum bent over backwards for him.

Katherine sighed as she left her office and locked the door behind her. Her heeled shoes echoed through the empty museum lobby as she made her way to the front door. Glad to see there were no protestors outside, she left the building and went to her car.

"What are you doing here?" she asked as she started the engine.

Picking up the gray stone orb that had secretly stowed itself away in her purse, she examined it. She set it back down in the empty cup-holder and sped off out of the parking lot trying to remember. She was sure she'd set it in the coaster on her large office desk between a stack of papers and her pen holder, but she couldn't for the life of her remember putting the thing in her purse.

◆

"You look absolutely divine," Ty said as he stood in her doorway dressed in tan slacks and a thick matching sweater. The black turtleneck he wore underneath made the color of his blue eyes and his lustrous blond hair stand out.

She glanced down at her white silk tank top matching her ruffled skirt lined with lace just above the knee and smiled. "Thank you. You don't look so bad yourself."

"I still can't believe you're finally going out with me," he said as he watched her lock her front door, leaning his palm on the brick exterior wall just above her head.

"We've gone out plenty of times, Ty," she replied, turning around to meet his gaze.

Feeling a bit awkward, she walked underneath his arm and headed for his car. He quickly caught up and fell into pace beside her.

"As true as it may be, this is the first time we've actually gone out on a real date."

"You know I'm not ready for us to be in a serious relationship."

"I know," he said with a shrug. "It doesn't mean we can't have a little fun together."

She watched him close the door and round to the driver's side.

He hurriedly jumped in, just giving her enough time to catch the scent of their dinner resonating from the picnic basket in the back seat.

"What did you bring?" she asked, grinning in fascination and the temptation of eating a hot meal.

For too long she'd lived off bagged salads and frozen meals. The quicker the meal, the more time she had to sculpt or paint. Except on the occasional outing with Ty, she stayed stuck in her little apartment, lost in her world of colors, clay and metal. So this was a real treat.

"Listen, dearest," Ty said as he shifted the gear into drive. "All you need to know is that I cooked. You're not the only good artist in town you know. It just so happens I went to a culinary school in Italy when I was twenty."

"So we're having spaghetti," she said with a smirk. There was always room for gloating when it came to him.

"Lasagna," he argued after seeing her unimpressed reaction. "I also made us some olive garlic bread to go with it."

"Sounds great," she said graciously.

She sat her purse down between her legs as he turned on the stereo. As a rush of classical music poured from the speakers, she caught a familiar shimmer in her eye, and it was coming from the floor of the car.

She glanced down with a scowl and a chill swept over her when she found the sparkling orb sitting inside the dark leather of her purse, slightly glowing.

"How did this get here?" she said as she picked it up in her hand and held it up.

"Isn't that the rock you found today?" Ty asked, turning the music down to a low whisper. "It's rather interesting in the sunlight, almost as if it's glowing, quite unusual."

Katherine agreed. She knew she should tell him it had made its way, by itself, into her purse before she left the museum, and once more before they left her apartment.

She remembered where she'd left it this time—on the dining table inside the decorative bowl of fake fruit.

It carried a slight glow, but this time it pulsated weakly as if it was trying to tell her something of importance. Was she going mad? Or could she possibly be seeing a truth nobody else seemed concerned about, especially the well-known archaeologist she was with now.

She shivered as she stuck the orb back inside her purse. What a ridiculous sentiment, she thought. To be fantasizing over nothing more than a perfectly round rock was amusing. A smile escaped her lips. She might as well be a young girl envisioning dragons flying through the sky, breathing fire on all the unsuspecting protestors sitting in the park they'd just pulled into.

"Just great," Ty said huffing in aggravation hoping their night wasn't ruined by demonstrations. "I should've known our romantic evening would be ruined by these fools."

Romance wasn't in the plans anyway, Katherine thought as they drove down the one lane road through the park. Admiring the protestors, she watched as they preached, holding picket signs about the coming Armageddon.

It was strange to see such a thing here in England. The people were so open-minded when it came to the paranormal. She'd driven through festivities that would scare the living daylights out of unsuspecting passersby. Entire blocks were cut off from normal traffic just for zombie fans to parade down streets showing off their horrifying, yet spirited mugs.

But a show of faith was here with them this evening. Maybe this was the other side of horror—a reality of religious fanatics and church extremists believing in Mother Ships and saving grace. These were the people to come and show what they truly feared, and according to their signs, it was the end of the world.

"Do they really think the devil's inside our box?" she asked Ty, watching as they passed a large group with a banner hanging over top of them. "Satan's Box," she read aloud.

Within the seriousness of her moment, she heard Ty start to laugh. She scowled at him, taking her eyes off the crowd slowly dissipating due to the sudden outburst from the sky.

Ty laughed again as they all scurried for the nearest shelter. "Serves them right," he said with an abundant grin. "Their idiocies are so backwoods. It's ridiculous."

"They're just scared," Katherine said.

"Scared of what?" Ty asked as he parked underneath an empty shelter. "Are they afraid it's the end of the world because we found an old coffin at the bottom of the Channel? Do you know how ridiculous it sounds for them to say we've found Satan in a bloody box?" He sighed. "It might as well be Pandora's."

"They're free to make their point. Just because you don't believe in God doesn't give you the right to judge how they feel."

"I suppose not," he replied. "I just don't understand how they get this from just a simple old artifact. I'd be the one to tell them the demon lord was inside, since I'm the expert."

He chuckled at his response and glanced over at her. He knew it was time to change the subject by the goaded look in her eye.

"I suppose this dinner will be fast food now."

He reached behind his seat and brought up the dark wooden basket lined with blue and white flannel cloth. Two wine baskets woven beautifully beside it were full with a bottle of red wine and two long-stemmed glasses.

"You aim to get me drunk?" she asked as he popped the cork on the bottle and poured her a glass.

"I would love to," he replied with a mischievous grin. "But I suppose I will be a gentleman tonight."

The rain tapered off into a light mist as he handed her an empty plate. He unsheathed the foil lining the glass dish of lasagna and suddenly realized he had nowhere to put it.

"I should have taken you to a fancy restaurant instead." He pouted.

She could tell his romantic night with her was beginning to sour and she suddenly felt sorry for him. He'd done so much work only to have it spoiled by wet grass and lack of car space.

She gripped her wine glass and grabbed the handle of the basket. She opened the car door and stepped out. Leaning down, she flashed him a smile, motioning with her head for him to join her on the pavement.

She sat down, placing the basket in front of her as he rounded the front of the car with a sigh. He set the bowl down on the ground and reached into the basket.

"Wa-la," he said as he pulled out a spatula, dug into the noodles, and placed a large heap on her plate along with a slice of garlic bread.

Set him free.

"Set who free?" Katherine asked, tossing Ty a questioning glance as she indulged in a bite.

He eyed her peculiarly. "What do you mean?"

"You asked me to set someone free," she replied.

"I didn't say anything."

Dismissing what she'd heard as nothing more than the trees rustling in the wind, she turned her attention back on her meal. She knew he didn't need any more encouragement to gloat, but the man truly had skills. The meal was perfect, right down to the last bite. And although she was full, if there were more on her plate, she'd eat it.

The sound of a horse clomping on pavement caught her ears. She peered overtop of the car and found a black carriage, pulled by a single brown horse, making its way towards them.

"I'm not sure about this," she said as she picked up her wine glass and leaned against the hood of the car. She watched Ty as he placed the basket in the back seat and walked toward her, holding his hand out for her to take.

"It'll be fun," he said grinning ear to ear. "Come on."

As they settled into the carriage, the driver watched. Dressed in a black tuxedo and a round fur-felt hat, he looked like a proper English gentleman.

He tapped the reins once and the horse began moving, pulling the carriage slowly along the one lane road. This was an interesting situation since Katherine had never experienced a carriage ride before. It was absolutely lovely, at least until they began riding through the regrouped protestors.

"Satan is among us!" She heard the preacher shout to the group of people, listening, shouting "amen" and holding up their signs. "Are you ready for the coming Apocalypse?"

The display sent chills down Katherine's spine. The driver tapped the reins harder, making the horse speed up.

Set him free, Katherine.

She turned to find out what Ty was whispering about again, but his head was turned the other way, staring at the protestors gathering on the other side of them.

"I think we should cut this ride short," she said, gathering Ty's attention to her worried eyes. "Something isn't right."

"What's wrong?" he asked.

"Could you please take us back to the car?" she asked the driver in a frantic voice.

You are the key, Katherine.

Her heart quickly pounded. Realizing Ty wasn't the one speaking to her, she sat forward.

"Please," she pleaded. "Stop the carriage!"

The driver did as she asked. She hopped down on the road and turned around, backing away as if a ghost lingered in front of her, watching her every move.

"What's wrong?" Ty asked, following her as she stepped back away.

"Sir," the driver said.

Ty acknowledged him, trying to keep his eye on Katherine as she stood in the grass pacing. "I'm sorry. I believe we're done for tonight."

She watched as the horse pulled the carriage away. Shaking her head, she let Ty take her by the hands.

"What happened just now?"

"I don't know," she replied. "I keep hearing this voice."

"A voice?" he asked a little surprised to hear it.

She gazed up into his worried face. As he looked at her, the thought of him thinking she was crazy crossed her mind. So with a reassuring sigh, she gave him a quaint fake smile.

"It's nothing. I guess I'm just a little stressed out about finishing this project." She knew she'd heard something, but the next time the voice came, she'd keep it to herself. "I'm sorry I ruined the carriage ride. Shall we go then?" she asked as she moved to the road, grazing his arm as she passed.

The confused look was prominent on his face as he stood there, watching her intently. But he quickly fell into pace beside her, and with a smooth move, took her by the hand and looped her arm through his.

She didn't mind it so much. It reassured her as they walked under the darkening sky along the road toward the car, watching as the protestors started to leave the park.

"Don't worry about them," Ty said, breaking the silence. "They have always loved this park. It has a long history of protestors and activists, coming to spread their word."

Katherine nodded, but didn't say anything. Still shaken by the voice she'd heard call her by name, she found herself holding tighter to his arm.

"Are you all right?" he asked. "Are you cold? You must be, you're shivering."

"I'm fine," she replied.

"Still wondering about the voice?" he asked, flashing a half-grin. "Talk to me Katherine."

"It's just stress," she answered.

"I know you too well, love. You heard something."

She stopped. With the car in sight, she felt safe knowing it was only a few more feet away if she had to run. Though thoroughly spooked, she knew she shouldn't be.

"Is it a man or woman's voice?" he asked, pulling her into his arms.

Normally she would object to being held by him, but for now she'd allow it. She leaned on him, folding her arms across her chest just for that extra space between them.

"It's a man's voice," she said, confessing. "He tells me to set him free. He whispered my name." She shivered and gave in to the temptation to wrap her arms around his torso.

He was warm and his body invited her as he held her close, but she turned slightly and started back toward the car with his arm still around her shoulders. Night had invaded the park, and it just made things much creepier.

"Sometimes people hear and see things that aren't really there on account of how stressed they are. So don't worry your pretty head." He kissed her lightly on the cheek. "You're not insane, dear."

"Where to now?" she asked as they made it back to the car.

"By now," he said. "We would have finished our hot cocoa as the carriage whisked us down the lamp-lit street. I would have confessed my love for you and hopefully stolen a few kisses from your sweet lips."

Katherine. The voice came and went with the cool breeze touching her face. She trembled, feeling as if whatever called her name watched her from behind.

She quickly turned her head and placed her eyes on the darkness at her back. And the tingle up her spine made her catch a short breath.

"Shall we go?" Ty asked, concern mingling in his soft voice.

"Yes," she answered hurrying into the passenger seat of the car.

Save me Katherine.

This was getting ridiculous. She reached over her shoulder and locked her door, but as she did, she caught a glimpse of glowing eyes outside her window, fading almost as soon as she saw them. Unable to hold in her fear any longer, she let out a blood-curdling scream, making Ty hurry into the driver's seat.

He slammed his door and immediately locked it. He quickly started the car, turned on the lights, and then shifted into gear.

"What the hell was that all about?" he asked, panting for breath as he sped out of the park and onto the lit street of the city.

"I thought I saw something," she said, covering her mouth with her hand, eyes wide. A relieving sigh escaped her as they drove under the lights.

"Well," he said, gathering his composure. "What did you see?"

She thought about it for a moment, debating on whether to tell him. It was just stress, she told herself. It was just a high amount of stress from her job that was taking way too long to finish.

"Nothing," she said with a wave of a nervous hand. "It was nothing."

"Come on," he said as they pulled up to the curb in front of her apartment. "Tell me what spooked you back there."

"I thought I saw," she started, but hesitated. "I thought I saw someone's eyes staring at me from outside my window."

He lowered his brows, turned off the engine, and leaned back in the seat. He sighed, obviously unprepared to comment.

"It's okay," she said palming the door handle, preparing to get out of the car.

"Wait," he said, grabbing her arm and stopping her from getting away. "I didn't mean to upset you."

"No," she said feeling a little awkward for telling him such a ridiculous thing. "Thank you for the lovely evening, Ty. I'm sorry I ruined it."

She pulled away from his grasp and got out of the car. Pulling her keys from her purse as she walked, she eyed the orb. An angry sensation built inside her as she stepped up to the door mindfully telling it to stop trying to frighten her with its eerie glow.

"I believe you," he said, walking up behind her. "But don't end our night yet."

She turned to face him, flashing an apologetic grin. "I think I just need to get some rest. The digging crew will be out early tomorrow morning. I need to be there to make sure everything goes okay."

"But it's only eight," he said. He swiped a lock of hair from her cheek and cupped her face. "Let me come in. I'll massage your shoulders."

As tempting as getting a massage was, she knew she couldn't allow him inside. She'd already given him the wrong message by letting him take her to the park.

Katherine.

This time the sound resonated from her purse. As Ty leaned down and kissed her on the cheek, she glanced down at the orb. The glow sent another chill up her spine.

"I'm sorry Ty," she said, pulling away from his wandering lips. "I'll see you tomorrow."

She hurriedly unlocked the door and went inside. Watching Ty's face sour as she shut the door on him, she couldn't help but feel sorry for him.

"What is going on?" she asked as she reached inside her purse and pulled the round nuisance out. She studied it carefully trying to figure out if she'd really seen it glowing just a few moments before, because it definitely wasn't now.

She couldn't forget the turquoise eyes in the dark. It was only a brief glance, but they were there. The voices she'd heard were real, so why hadn't Ty heard them?

She slumped down into her small brown couch and kicked off her shoes. As she stared at the orb, glittering in the low light of the room, her eyes became heavy. But before she could fall asleep, she heard a familiar little squeak.

"There you are, you little scavenger," she whispered, squinting her eyes at the small figure standing in the middle of the hardwood floor.

The mouse she'd been trying to catch for a month seemed to laugh at her, taunting her into making a move, just like she had so many times before. She'd failed to catch him no matter what she tried to use.

Mousetraps, he outsmarted them. Sticky paper never caught anything but a few small bugs. It was deemed impossible, for she'd run out of ideas. Though she refused to get poison, the decision to buy some was drawing close. And what she was seeing now made the decision much easier.

She smirked as she watched it eat cheese from its front paws. It was the same cheese she'd attached to the mousetrap the night before. He'd somehow managed to free it without getting caught. "Smart little thing, aren't you?" she said. "But I'll get you sooner or later."

It sat up, staring at her with such an odd intensity as it ate. It was strange. As if it understood what she'd just said, it gave out a small squeak then scurried away, disappearing underneath the refrigerator.

She lay back, feeling rather exhausted. Extending her legs along the length of the couch, she sighed, palm to forehead, and before long, fell asleep.

Chapter Two

The same dream came the night before. The white horse matching her flowing gown galloped proudly across the field. On bareback it was easy to ride, powerful between her legs, and hair soft as silk. Nothing could describe its beauty, its elegance.

She was too inferior to be riding such a beast. With tears streaming her pale cheeks, she'd sensed its sadness. The turmoil it had endured was great, bringing death by the hand of someone dear to its heart.

Who could be evil enough to murder such a marvelous being? she'd thought as she easily slid off its back and onto the solid stone steps of the temple.

She stepped up and found herself again bowing to someone with long flowing black hair. A man dressed in white clothing reached out to her with a burning palm, but if only she could see his face.

"Katherine." She heard Ty's voice calling from outside her office door.

Shaking off the visions of her dream, she swiveled from the construction crew working outside her window. She hadn't seen Ty all morning and it was near noon already. "Come in," she said as she stood up, preparing to go outside and inspect the excavation.

The door slowly opened and his friendly face peered through the crack. He smiled sweetly, but she could tell he was nervous.

"I thought maybe you'd like to go to lunch," he spoke like it were a confession, or maybe even an apology.

"I'd love to," she replied, twisting her lips slightly to the side. "But I need to be here when they put the arch in the ground, which should be anytime now."

Ty nodded, showing himself into the office. With his hands in his pockets she could tell he really wanted to talk about their date last night, but she didn't want to go there.

"Maybe we can do lunch tomorrow," she continued, grabbing her brown leather jacket off the back of her chair.

She put it on and headed toward the door, but he caught her by the hand before she could walk out. Pursing her lips, she turned to argue, but he shushed her with his finger.

"I know what you're going to say," he said lowering his brow in seriousness. "You're going to tell me you have no feelings for me at all, especially after last night. Not that I blame you. I am quite pig-headed. What I'm trying to say is I'm sorry. I shouldn't have been so cheap." He glanced down at her chin as he placed his hands on her shoulders. "Just give me another chance. Let me make it up to you."

She gave a short breath through her nose. "Ty, I just don't think we're meant to be. I love our relationship the way it is now. It's simple. I don't want to ruin what we have."

He nodded, obviously trying to agree with her, but his eyes told her differently. He wasn't going to accept it.

"Listen," he continued. "Simple has never been in my vocabulary. Just give me one more date to show you how I truly am. I won't try so hard this time."

Katherine thought for a moment. The way he looked into her eyes, pleading and weighing on her pity. It was sickening and amusing.

"Fine," she said knowing she'd regret it. "One more date, but I don't think it will change the way I feel."

"Thank you," he said with a relieving sigh. "I'm going to lunch. We'll go over details later."

"Fine," she said as he turned and left the office.

With a quick glance out the window, she realized the workers had left for lunch as well. Aggravated they'd stopped before they set the arch, she quickly walked from her office and out the side door. Running her eyes over the dug up earth, she sighed.

Finding her way into the cobblestone courtyard, she slowly circled the pond, trying desperately not to make eye contact with the coffin sitting on the altar above her. An ominous presence hovered thick in the air and an eerie sensation crept over her as if it called to her, but there were no voices this time.

She stopped her dawdling march and turned to face the pond.

With eyes on the concrete wall, she kicked off her shoes and made her way to it.

Unsure if it was by force or on her own accord, she carefully stepped up onto the wall. She crossed the cold pond, getting the bottom of her mauve flower print skirt wet.

Careful not to disturb the loose brick before the altar, she climbed the short steps until she stood face to face with whatever had called her there. Glancing at the markings, it beckoned her to touch them with her fingers.

Sliding them sensually over the lid, she closed her eyes. A strong sensation of sadness burrowed deep inside her heart, making her feel like all hope was lost.

"I'm sorry," she whispered through guilty sobs. "I'm so sorry." Falling weak, she slid down to her knees and leaned on it. It became warm to the touch as her fingers traced a small indention near the edge where she sat.

She opened her tear-filled eyes acknowledging the space wasn't there when she'd studied it with Ty, but it was definitely there now. Wiping her tears, she stood up and inspected it closely.

It was a perfect circle, big enough for a softball to sit in. She looked over at her window. Or it was big enough for the orb.

A piece must have broken off without anyone knowing. This ancient artifact, a priceless piece, had most likely been hit by the careless workers during their excavation. The orb had fallen to the ground, and would have been buried in concrete if she hadn't found it.

Angry, Katherine tromped through the pond uncaringly getting her skirt wet. She hopped off the concrete wall and found her shoes.

Ready to go have a word with the head of the excavation team, she made her way toward the entry door, wringing out the bottom of her skirt.

Katherine.

The call of her name stopped her from opening the large glass door. She knew now where the voice came from. And it was then she knew in her heart that someone or something was locked inside the box. And it desperately wanted out.

"I hold the key," she whispered, remembering what he'd said to her before. "And the key is the orb."

A sick feeling billowed in the pit of her stomach, making her terribly dizzy. She hurriedly made her way to her office with her face in her hands. And when she sat down in her high back chair, she stared out the window.

"What am I going to do?" she asked herself aloud.

She should tell Ty about this. The museum should know she was holding the key to opening this box, but envisioning Armageddon, she shivered. What if the protestors were right? What if Satan was locked away inside that thing, and he was luring her to set him free?

She swiveled away from the window and shivered again. Her body trembled all over at the thought she would be the one to unleash hell upon earth. A demon would crawl out and with his evil hand, strike down every human he found, including the one who released him.

She couldn't do it. There was just no way she was prepared to face the consequences. No matter how tempting it was or how much the voice pleaded with her, she would not unlock the box.

She quickly picked up the orb and stuffed it inside the bottom drawer of her desk. With a quick step, she left the room and made her way out front. Her breath was frantic as if she'd just sprinted miles. And trying to catch it, she leaned over the railing.

Voices caught her ears, loud and angry—chanting. They were coming closer, heading her way. Protestors were marching down the sidewalk toward the museum holding signs with pictures of Satan, images of red demons with horns and forked tongues.

Do not fear me, Katherine.

The voice, whispering in her ear, made her panic. A dizzy spell crept over her as she stumbled for the front door, trying not to fall. But she couldn't hold out any longer as she lost her footing and headed for the floor.

Strong arms caught her before she fell. He lifted her off her feet and carried her into her office where he lay her down on the black leather couch along the wall. With soft strokes, he brushed her hair from her face.

"You carry the gem," she heard a deep voice say, causing her to shiver. "The orb is the key to unlocking my soul." His voice was of passion, strength, and unbelievable love. And she longed to hear more, but it unfortunately faded into a sweet British accent she knew all too well.

"Katherine," Ty said, patting her lightly on the cheek.

"What happened?" she mumbled as she opened her eyes.

"I think you fainted," he replied. "Are you okay?"

"Yeah," she said as she sat up in the couch.

"Want me to get you a glass of water?"

"No," she replied. "I'm fine."

Finding equilibrium, she rose to her feet and began to pace, glancing out the window. The men had started working again, and she watched as two of them held the arch in their hands as another poured concrete into the hole.

It was beautiful. Only half done, it was already starting to take shape in her eyes. One high arch curved to the right of the box, and the other sat low to the left.

She tried to deny her vision as she stared, but it had come to her too quickly. Once the twisted metal pieces were up, the finished design would look like a large metal horse.

With her hand over her mouth, she gasped. The sick feeling in her stomach came once again. But this time, her fear was interrupted.

Ty placed his hands on her shoulders and gently squeezed. Instead of fighting it, she closed her eyes and welcomed his comforting touch.

"I'm worried about you," he said, his breath in her ear. "Are the voices troubling you again?"

"You talk as though you think I'm crazy," she said in a calm voice as she moved back to her desk.

He tried reassuring her, but it wasn't working. Instead she became agitated as she fumbled through the drawer, frantically searching for the orb until she found it.

"Look at this," she scolded, grasping it in her hand. She held it up for him to see. "This is the key to unlocking the box."

"How do you know?" he asked, taking it from her grasp.

"The voice told me." She rolled her eyes knowing how ridiculous it sounded.

With a puzzling glance, he inspected the orb. "The voice told you this rock is the key?"

"Yes."

"I didn't see anything on the box resembling this shape."

"But I found where it fits."

"When?"

"Today," she replied.

They exchanged glances for a moment. Katherine held her breath, knowing she'd finally sparked his interest.

Grasping the ball in his hand, Ty gave her a half grin. "Show me."

She led him outside. Her fear suddenly turned to excitement as she guided him through the fish pond and up to the box.

"It's here," she said, running her hand over the surface. She'd felt it there before, she was sure of it. But now, there was nothing but a smooth surface.

"I don't understand," she said, searching with her fingers.

Ty began searching as well. "Are you sure?"

"I'm positive. It was right here not more than an hour ago."

"Maybe you were dreaming."

"No," she snapped angrily. "It was real."

"Listen Katherine," Ty said as he stood straight, giving up his search. "You were pretty out of it earlier. Maybe you imagined it."

She sat down on the altar steps, letting her feet dangle in the pond. Ty sat down beside her and handed her back the orb with a sigh.

"I'm sorry," she said, shaking her head in disappointment.

"Ah, don't worry about it." He put his arm around her shoulder and pulled her close. "We all go through periods of exhaustion. Maybe you just need a rest."

"Maybe," she replied as he stood to his feet and waded back through the pond.

"Are you coming back in?" he asked as he jumped down onto the cobblestone path.

"I'll be there in a moment."

She watched him leave knowing he was disappointed, though there was no doubt in her mind something was there before. Running her fingers over the surface, she found it smooth. No indentions, no strange voices, and no emotional outbreaks came this time. It was just a simple, ancient metal box sitting coolly under her art.

Taking one last glance at the orb, she oddly said goodbye as if it were a living being. She set it down on the box and then stepped down into the cool water ready to forget all about it. But as she stepped across the pond, it rolled across the top and teetered slightly on the edge.

With a squinted eye, she watched until she was sure it wasn't going to fall in the water. What did it matter anyway, she thought. It didn't hold any value to her design or to the box. It was just an unusual rock. At least it's what she forced herself to believe as she hesitantly left it sitting on the edge.

Chapter Three

People stared at him as he walked down the sidewalk beside the busy city street. Long black hair, still damp from sea water, stretched down his back. His pale naked body seemed to glow underneath the lamp lights.

They walked around him, some scowling at his presence, some catching a snicker or two. A small group of women gathered near him, whispering, giggling amongst each other as they watched him stop and stare in a window, mesmerized by the modern clothing hanging marvelously on a mannequin.

Flashing a short grin at the ladies, he went inside the shop, ignoring the outburst of playful growls and catcalls he received from them. A man dressed in a dark suit and a wide silver tie walked up to him, grinning ear to ear. His mustache looked as if it had been drawn over the top of his lip with a fine red ballpoint pen. And his matching hair was in perfect long spikes around the top of his head.

He pointed at the tag on the leaf of his suit. "My name is Pierre," he said with a shy grin and ran his eyes down the bare body standing before him. "And oh my goodness, you need some clothes don't you?"

Pierre's voice was friendly. Though he had a slight lisp when he talked, his English was proper. His nose puckered showing he was quite miffed about something, or possibly quite intrigued.

"If the fashion police were here, I'd have them arrest you for breaking the law! You have the body of a God, if I may say." The man held his forefinger curled to his lips, obviously in thought. He arched his brows and smiled richly. "I know just the outfit for a man of your stature."

A black long sleeve shirt hung on the rack behind Pierre. He quickly pulled it off the bar and slung it daintily over his arm. Eyeing black slacks on the other side of the small well-lit store, he motioned him to follow.

"Do you have a name, Sir?" Pierre asked as he eloquently pulled a dark pair of argyle socks and silk boxers off the rack as they passed.

"Name?" he asked, frowning as he intensely thought. "My name is Sir." He gave Pierre a confused grin.

"Sir?" Pierre stood before him, puckering his nose again as he lifted the black slacks off the bar. "No, no. You obviously look more like a Dirk or a Derrick, especially with your dark hair and those ... eyes. Your skin is also very pale."

Pierre lowered his brows, giving him another long stare, but the puzzled look soon morphed back into his usual puckered, bright-eyed grin.

"Suntans are so overrated anyway," he sighed. "Come with me. You can try these on in the fitting room. I'm telling you this is the perfect outfit for you. All this black will bring out those sea-green eyes." Pierre hesitated again, ogling avidly at him. "I'm sorry for staring, but they really are the most beautiful eyes I've ever seen. They're so bright."

Pierre blushed as he quickly led him to the back of the store. "I have a friend who lives upstairs. He can style your hair for you if you like. Long hair is out now. However, it does work for you, but I'd suggest a long layer, maybe a style over your ears and eyes, though I wouldn't cover such beauty if I were you. You could be bald and still look rather ravenous."

He walked through a cream colored drapery door and into the fitting room. He laid out the clothes on the bench inside and smiled with a sigh.

"I'll go get him now, and we can get your hair styled for you before you leave."

Pierre turned his head, trying his best not to look as he shut the curtain. "Oh my," he whispered, taking the handkerchief from his breast pocket and fanning his face with it. Turning a slight shade of pink at seeing the handsome broad physique of his customer, he smiled running to the back room calling for his friend.

•

He stood staring in the mirror at the black shoes on his feet.

He didn't like them at all. They hurt his toes in an odd way. But confined to the clothes this strange man named Pierre had picked out for him, he knew he'd now blend in on the streets, making his purpose a little less conspicuous.

Putting the leather jacket on, he smiled at his quite handsome reflection. His hair was trimmed slightly, but styled clean by Pierre's friend who still watched him from the other side of the room, smiling and waving whenever he glanced over.

Such strange men, he thought, though glad they had helped him.

Pierre stood behind him offering him a breathtaking sigh. "You are perfect, except you have your shoes on the wrong feet." He giggled like a girl. "Sit down, I'll help you."

The recliner beside the mirrors was comfortable. As Pierre switched the shoes to the proper foot, Derrick stared at himself in the mirror.

Derrick, he thought. The name fit him well, at least until he could remember his real one. He hoped his mission would be quick so he wouldn't have to use it for too long.

His feet felt much better. With a smile and a nod, he stood back up and inspected himself again.

"That's better, yes?" Pierre asked intently, grazing his eyes over him. "You are a masterpiece. Have you ever thought about modeling? I know this guy who works for an agency downtown that would just die to see you in print."

"Thank you for your help, Pierre," he replied, slowly sounding out the first sentence he'd spoken in many years. Single words were a cinch, but it would take a while to catch up to speaking this language again. "I will not need modeling," he continued. "There are important tasks I must do."

It was the first time he saw Pierre frown. It didn't suit the small frilly man, but as usual he shrugged it off and returned his smile. He walked behind the small store counter and began pushing buttons on the register. "This will be fifteen hundred pounds. Will it be cash or credit?"

"Cash or Credit?"

"You need to pay for these clothes and your hairstyle. You can pay, can't you?" Pierre rolled his eyes as he remembered the man had come in stark naked. He smiled diligently, giving him a wicked eye. "Oh, don't worry your pretty head. I'll just put it on a tab and you can pay me whenever you can."

"You need money," he said as he pulled a large wad of bills from the pocket of his new pants and gave it to Pierre. "This should be enough?"

"Oh my, yes," Pierre said, arching his brow in fascination at all the bills rolled loosely together. "How did …?" he started to ask, but decided not to as the man started to leave. "Wait," he called after him. "You never told me your name."

"My name is Derrick for now."

"Come back and see me, Derrick for now. I'll find you a new outfit when you wear that one out."

Derrick walked out of the store. He glanced back at Pierre who stood in the doorway waving with tears in his eyes.

Strange indeed, he thought as he made his way down the city street. Feeling confident he was appropriately dressed for this strange new world, he was ready to finally do his bidding. Though he wasn't sure where to start, for everything around him was new. He stopped at a window, amazed by the magic images coming to life on glass surfaces. Intrigued, he watched it curiously for a long moment until the store owner reached over and made it stop. The man shrugged at him and pointed at his watch to let him know he was closing for the night.

Though he wanted to see more, he continued down the street. It seemed everything shut down at the same time. Owners turned their closed signs to him as he passed, until one by one, all the lights in the buildings on the street were off.

Traffic thinned as he continued walking. People were no longer with him. And now completely alone, memories from his past whirled in his mind.

He saw blood on his hands, seeping into his skin and causing them to burn with an intense fire. Tears of rage bore vividly in his mind as he took the life of his dearest friend. He'd memorized the sadness in her eyes as he struck her down and stole the very essence of her life. Why had he done such a despicable thing?

He stopped on the street. Finding reality once more, he turned to face a small building. He breathed in a familiar luring scent and closed his eyes.

It was her—the one from his dreams. Her heart had unleashed

him from his eternal suffering, from his eternal loneliness. And it would be her heart that would hopefully guide him home.

Chapter Four

Night had come fast for Katherine. After leaving the museum that evening, she felt miserable. Maybe it had something to do with leaving the orb sitting on the blasted coffin.

She was sick of it—sick of hearing things not there, sick of seeing those unbelievable eyes glowing, staring at her every time she closed hers. Tired of feeling a fear of unleashing something evil into the world, or the fact she was just going crazy, she decided on taking her misery to the pub down the street from her apartment.

After her fourth shot of warm whiskey, her vision blurred. She began talking to the man next to her, and he was enjoying every bit of her conversation about vacationing on a secluded beach with a nudist colony.

"There I was, covering my front and back with one of those fold-up chairs," she said, slurring her words. "I felt like everyone was staring at me." She laughed. "But the funny thing was that I was the one staring, and it didn't make a bit of difference to them."

"So did you stay? Or did you turn your gorgeous tail around and jet out of there?"

"I stayed," she said proudly. "I actually ended up enjoying it." She sighed as she thought aloud. "It was kind of like walking in the footsteps of Eve."

"Eve?" he asked curiously.

"You know," she said as she stood up. "Biblical times, Adam and Eve." Dizziness swept through her and she slightly lost her footing. Realizing she definitely wasn't sober enough to be talking to anyone about anything, she patted him on the shoulder.

"I think I'll head home now," she said. "Thanks for the chat."

"Want me to walk you home, Love?" he asked with a raised brow. "I don't think you're going to make it."

"I'll be fine," she said with a grin.

She made her way to the door. Glancing at her watch as she walked out, she sighed. It was almost one AM and she had a lot of work to do the next day. She was going to regret drinking so much.

As she started up the walkway with a swerve to her step, she heard the door to the pub open and close. Footsteps fell into stride behind her, and the same man she'd just talked to called out to her.

"Hey, wait up."

A chill worked over her as he fell into pace beside her. He may have been there to listen to her babble, but she wasn't interested in him following her home.

"You don't need to walk me," she said, quickening her pace.

The man caught her by the arm. He held tight as he walked with her, enforcing his stride until they came to the alley just before her apartment.

"Let go of me," she argued, trying to pull away from his hurtful grasp. "I'll scream."

He laughed as he forced her down the alley. She started to scream for help, but he quickly pulled her around and clasped his hand over her mouth.

"Shut up!" he growled in her ear.

His breath stunk of stale booze as he pressed his lips to her cheek. She felt something sharp on her neck and realized he was holding a knife to her throat. Tears immediately came to her eyes at the thought her life was in his hands.

"Where's your house?" he asked, slightly lifting his grasp on her mouth so she could talk.

"It's up the walkway," she answered. Her vision glazed as he pushed her toward the street.

"Don't get any ideas about screaming," he said with the knife at her back. "Just walk like you know me."

She led him up the street, constantly feeling the point on her skin. Desperately trying not to stumble back into it, she held her blurry gaze to the ground.

"What are you going to do to me?"

"Just get us to your house. I'll take anything valuable you got."

This shouldn't be happening, she thought as she burst into a cry, wishing she'd stayed home for the night. "I don't own anything valuable."

"Just keep moving," the man said as he twisted the blade in her back.

She heard her dress rip and a sharp pain hit her. Nausea set in and the reality of what was happening took a terrifying form.

As she started up the short steps to her front door, she cried. Trembling in fear, she unlocked the door and opened it. He shoved her aside and walked in, blade held in front of him in case someone else was there.

It was her chance to run as he left her standing in the doorway to search through her apartment. And as she backed slowly away, the scenario played in her head. She'd run to the bar and plead for help. Someone would call the police as she called Ty to come stay with her for she refused to be alone tonight.

She trembled as she turned to run. Fearing he'd follow, she kept her eyes on the door. But when she took her first step, she walked straight into someone's arms.

In fear, she raised her glance to the most remarkable thing she'd ever seen in her life. Turquoise eyes shining brightly from the light of the room behind her, gazed down into her tear-filled stare.

For a moment she was lost as he held her, watching with such intensity she felt she'd plunged into the sea. But the slam of the door to her room brought her back to her senses.

The thief had found her bedroom and was pulling her jewelry from the box on her dresser. Her gold bracelet and pendant necklace among the dozen pieces she'd collected since she was a child, was all about to be stolen away, ending in some pawn shop.

The man holding her broke away from his lingering glance. He stepped around her and went inside the apartment.

She backed down the steps, clutching the long sleeves of her dress in her hands as she heard the thief shout loudly. A chair tipped over into the floor and a few glasses shattered in the kitchen, making her flinch.

The new stranger held the back of her attacker's neck in his hand, escorting him forcefully and quite easily from the apartment. The thief dropped the bag from his hand, cursing under strained breath. And after he was shoved to the ground, he scrambled to his feet and sprinted down the street, shouting profanities.

Katherine didn't know what to do. Tears flowed from her eyes as she fell to her knees and pulled the thief's black garbage bag open. She found all of her jewelry, a stash of money she'd hidden away for a rainy day, and lo and behold, the orb she'd left on the coffin at the museum.

The stranger pulled the bag from her hands, and casually opened it. He oddly dug through it as if looking for something specific.

"Where is the diamond?" he asked curiously worried.

"It's safe," she replied clenching her fist. "I can't believe this," she said as she wiped tears angrily from her cheeks.

"Are you hurt?" her rescuer asked, offering his hand for her to take.

She hesitated, scowling at him. Though he looked innocent and perfectly handsome in his black suit, she was unsure of his intentions. But with a sigh, she gave him her hand and he helped her up to her feet.

"It's a sobering moment to be held at knife-point," she said crossly as she stormed into her apartment wiping more tears from her eyes. "I sincerely thought it was my moment to die."

He watched her intently from the doorway as she moved from living room to kitchen, replacing everything the ingrate stole from her. "You saved my life," she said as he stepped inside and shut the door behind him. "If it wasn't for you, it's hard to tell what might have happened. Thank you."

"I am glad to help you," he said, flashing a beautiful grin.

He gave his head a quick toss, removing a lock of hair from his eyes. And she suddenly allowed herself to be caught in them again.

"I must say," she said as she walked his way. "Your timing was impeccable. Were you just passing by?"

He thought for a moment, and she could see his struggle for an answer. He was absolutely stunning to look at, though somehow she could tell his agenda was less than coincidence.

"Tell me the truth," she said, stopping within an arm's length of him.

"I am looking for a woman named Katherine."

A chill worked down her spine when he said her name. His deep voice seemed familiar, but she couldn't for the life of her remember where she'd heard it.

She set the empty bag down on the kitchen table and picked up the chair from the floor, quickly setting it in place under the table before she returned his glance. He stood as still as a board, but his eyes seemed to melt into hers, and a strange sensation worked over her. Her heart lightly pounded in her ears, tossing her unusually into relaxation.

Her eyes became heavy, and she knew a coming sleep was evident. She needed to find her bed and lie down, but her eyesight was fading fast.

It was as if everything slowed to the sound of her heart as she fell toward the floor. She watched it come as if it were a blurred dream. This wasn't the outcome of her drunken state—this was something completely different.

His strong arms caught her once again and he held her close, pressing her body gently against him. It was an arousing sensation and her breath was lost in the moment as he lifted her and carried her into the bedroom.

He laid her gently down on the bed and covered her with the blanket. She wanted to scream at him and tell him to leave her alone, but she hadn't the strength or will to do it. Completely pervious to what he had planned for her, she could only hope this enchanting stranger wasn't going to turn out to be worse than the last.

He pressed his finger to her lips, quieting her fear of him into a deeper state of unconsciousness. And as if he read her mind, he pulled away and stood up.

"I will see you in the morning."

She watched him walk out, and shut the bedroom door behind him, leaving her in her dark room. This man, this perfectly beautiful man, held secrets behind his eyes. She could somehow sense sadness in them, even after just a few brief glances. It was as if she'd known him all her life, but had never seen him before until now.

And as she drifted off to sleep, she began to dream her same dream. But this time, she wasn't alone on her powerful white stallion. This time, her savior rode with her.

Chapter Five

A loud screeching noise came from the kitchen, waking Katherine. It gave her terrible chills as if someone ran fingernails down a chalkboard.

She jumped from the bed and ran to the door, frantic something was horribly wrong in her apartment, but the noise suddenly stopped. Thankful it had, she swung the door open and cautiously made her way out into the kitchen.

He sat at the table drinking a glass of water, staring out the window at the passing traffic. She remembered him from the night before, and from her dream that ended peculiarly erotic. A tinge of rose showed in her cheeks as she came to stand before him, trying not to show interest.

"You know I appreciate your help last night, but I never invited you to stay the night in my house."

He turned his gaze from the window, eyeing her with those unbelievable gems. It was as if he burned a hole through her act of disliking him as she found herself hung up on him once again.

"What was that noise?" she asked as she turned to make a pot of coffee, yet still keeping her eye on him.

"A mouse went underneath your cold box."

Embarrassed he'd seen her little annoying friend, she sighed. "I've been trying to get rid of it for quite some time now. But it seems to outwit all the traps I leave for it."

"He won't come back."

"Oh." Katherine was surprised to hear it. "Did you catch him?" She washed her favorite mug and then pulled another from the shelf.

"He told me it was blocking his hole in the floor. He has been trying to tell you since you moved in, but you do not listen. So I moved it for him."

He took another drink of his water, ignoring the confused glance she gave him as he turned his eyes back to the window. Though intrigued by what he said, she didn't know whether to laugh at his joke, or kick him out of her apartment for being completely insane.

"You spoke to a mouse?" she asked, trying to find humor in it.

"Yes. He rather likes you, but feels you do not enjoy his company."

"You can say that again," she mumbled, ignoring he'd answered in a serious voice.

She turned her attention to the steaming teapot and lifted it off the burner. She grabbed the cream out of the refrigerator trying to forget about his comment, but surprisingly found a smile over it. It was actually a sweet sentiment though a tad strange.

"Do you like your coffee black or with cream?" she asked, glancing back at him, catching his stare.

"I will have what you have, Katherine," he replied.

Ignoring the odd way he looked at her, she handed him her favorite mug. The scent of coffee and vanilla permeated the air and she enjoyed watching him breathe it in with a smile. It wasn't until he gulped it down did the situation change.

"It's very hot," she warned a little too late as he let out a deep horrified gurgle. Coffee streamed out of his mouth and dripped down his chin. And when he stood up, tipping the chair over into the floor, he covered his mouth with his hand.

Katherine quickly handed him his water. Accepting it without hesitation, he drank it down, dousing the flames on his tongue.

"Are you okay?" she asked worriedly.

"I am fine," he said, choking slightly and trying to present another grin. His eyes watered as he picked up the chair and sat back down at the table.

"Haven't you ever had coffee before?" she asked as she sat down in the chair on the other side of him.

When he shook his head, she stared at him. She could tell now he wasn't from London, or any big city for that matter. He was a little slow, especially with the way he spoke, as if he were a foreigner only knowing simple words. Realizing he may have wandered away from an institution, she decided she'd call around and find out where he belonged.

"You never told me your name," she said.

"Derrick."

"Derrick," she repeated curiously. "Do you have a last name?"

"Another name?" he asked, arching his brows. "Do I need one?"

"Most people do, but I suppose it's okay if you don't," she said, playing along. "Where exactly are you from?" she asked, hoping she could get a straight answer from him and save her from doing all the work. "You've never had coffee before. You say the strangest things, not to mention you can talk to mice. Please, enlighten me."

Entranced in his eyes, she felt his sadness again. And although he smiled at her, she could tell he had no idea what to say.

He flashed his smile and took a small sip of his coffee before he answered. "This is good now that I know how to drink it."

"Don't change the subject," she scolded. "Who are you?"

He eyed her curiously, and then took her by the hand. He rose to his feet, pulling her with him until they were face to face, and then he wrapped his arms around her shoulders.

"I will show you all things, but it is time to awaken."

Katherine frowned at his sudden prophetic voice. She pulled away from his grasp and backed away. "What things?"

"I must see your thoughts, Katherine," he continued as he slowly walked toward her with a half-grin. "Teach me so I will see the world with your eyes, for I cannot remember my full purpose."

"Get out of my house," she said, glaring at him as he backed her against the wall. He quickly leaned down with the intent to kiss her, but she wasn't going to allow it. With all her strength, she'd fight this handsome stranger off.

Anxiety billowed through her. Her heart quickened as he quickly pressed his lips to hers. Hands to his chest, she pushed as hard as she could, but he wouldn't budge. His strength was incredible, unusual. His power over her began to take precedence and she finally gave up the fight. She had no choice but to be kissed.

She welcomed the temptation knowing this was against her will. Sliding her arms around his neck, she conformed to the strange arousing feeling and gave him everything she had.

It was amazing as she desperately wanted him to leave, but would give anything to make him stay. He had become even stranger than before, yet somehow she was compelled by him, lost in him, weak for his touch. And when he broke away from their kiss, she wanted more.

The mysticism of his eyes, glowing astoundingly, made her catch her breath. It was as if he penetrated her thoughts and desires, gazing into her soul, finding truth in her deepest, darkest secrets.

Her eyes began to burn, finding them hard to close, for his stare pierced hers with overwhelming intensity. Her head ached as he drove deep, digging into all of her memories—of her childhood being tossed from one home to another, and the elderly woman that took her in when she was eight, and then died soon after, leaving her again to a social nightmare of homes.

He made her think of her black diamond, forcing her to show him where she kept it. Since her earliest memory, she'd carried the gem in the palm of her hand, stuck perfectly as if somehow it clung by an invisible adhesive. Knowing there was something special about it, she was unable to let go. It had brought her comfort in her darkest times, and somehow believed it linked her to something important.

Her head intensely throbbed, but it quickly dissipated as a pleasuring sensation fell over her. Breathing a sigh of relief, she found herself inside her recent dream, riding across rolling hills on the white stallion, holding onto this perfect stranger.

He led her up the stone steps of a temple where arousal came to the brink of ecstasy as she found his hands around her waist, intensely massaging. He made love to her, and the movement of their bodies was exhilarating, pleasure was bountiful, but she knew this wasn't real.

Katherine pulled from his hold on her, breaking away from his gaze. She immediately fell to the floor, trembling as she crawled across the kitchen catching her erratic breath.

"What just happened?" she asked in a pant, trying to shake the orgasmic sensation as she horrifyingly stared into the fading glow of his eyes.

He'd somehow made her relive her entire life and her passionate dreams. All the key points, tragedy, celebrations—sexual desires, he'd dug them from her mind and watched them like a sick movie. And now the dreams she'd been having were no longer hers.

With his pleasured grin, she could tell he enjoyed sensing them.

She rose to her feet, massaging her temple as she stumbled away from him. But her attempt fell short as he grabbed her arms and held her rigid before him.

"Your life is passionate, and your dreams are so vivid. It was incredibly beautiful, Katherine," he said, his speech much clearer than before.

His tone caught her attention, and she suddenly became afraid. "Please, let me go," she said, whispering in a strangled voice. "I don't know who or what you are, but you don't belong here."

"Don't be afraid of me." He grinned, straightening his poise. His eyes were vexed, much more than they should be, but he released his grasp on her arms. "I can't leave yet," he continued as he sat down at the kitchen table and gave out a confident sigh. "Now that I can actually think straight, it will be much simpler to discuss."

"Who are you?" she asked through whispering sobs. "What do you want from me?"

He watched her cry as she crept along the wall, terrified of him. Tears had smeared her makeup, leaving her eyes black, and her cheeks stained the same dreadful color.

"I need your help." His voice was proper, but still deep and haunting in her ears, as if he spoke another language and somehow she understood.

The phone rang, and her eyes left his gaze. Slowly sliding her way along the wall toward it, she was glad he made no attempt to stop her. And when she picked up the receiver, she answered in a trembling voice.

"Katherine, where are you?" Ty's voice beamed in her ear. "You were due here an hour ago. I have some absolutely astounding news!"

She could hear the excitement in his voice. Commotion rang out behind him and she wondered what the fuss was all about.

"What's going on?" she asked, watching Derrick closely as he began to roam around her apartment. With his hands clasped behind his back, he looked as if he were waltzing through an art gallery.

"You were right," he said excitedly. "The indention was there. I don't know why I didn't see it before. It's like it magically appeared."

"What was inside?" she asked curiously, knowing what the

answer would be.

"Sea water," Ty replied solemnly. "And I'm sorry to say your goldfish were eaten by some sort of Piranha."

Her heart broke when she heard the goldfish she'd personally picked for the pond were dead. "Where in the world did they come from?"

"It's going to sound ridiculous, but I think they were inside the coffin."

"It's not possible."

"I know," he agreed. "It's perfectly absurd, but it's true."

A moment of silence went by and she debated on whether to tell him about her eventful night. But when she saw Derrick eyeing her impatiently, she decided to keep it to herself.

She ended the call with Ty, and began to wonder how Derrick's eyes were able to glow. She wondered how they'd penetrated her so intently. There had to be some sort of explanation for it, possibly a drug he'd given her—maybe lingering on his lips before he kissed her, but definitely not some being from an ancient box full of sea water and flesh-eating fish.

Anger washed over her at the thought. He'd rescued her the night before just to attack her mind. Who knows, she shrugged, maybe the entire night was planned just to get her belongings, which really weren't worth much anyway. But the black diamond, she raised her hand and inspected the gem. Nobody would take this from her—it meant too much.

She moved into the kitchen, cringing as her dress rubbed against the place in her back where the man had held his knife. As she touched it with her fingers, she began to worry if she needed to go to the hospital for a tetanus shot and a blood test.

"Let me see," Derrick demanded, turning her around before she could decline. "Take down your dress and let me have a look." He grinned mischievously.

She turned her back to him. And before she could stop herself, she pulled her arms out of the long sleeves of her dress and hesitantly pulled down the top, covering her breasts with her arm.

"You're forcing me do this, aren't you?" she hesitantly asked, though it sounded perfectly unreasonable.

She should fear him, and the thought played on her mind like a grim overture. But when he delicately touched her, the fear morphed into gentle longing.

He made her skin rise, running his fingers over the small of her back, she shivered. "He didn't break the skin," he said in a soothing voice, but one strong and capable of luring her into wanting him closer.

"Good," she said slipping her arms back in her sleeves as he moved away. Though thankful he did, she was slightly disappointed.

She knew she should tell Ty about him, but he was too much of a pessimist to believe. And even if he did, he'd be the first to leave him on a table, cut up into pieces and studied for possible ways to make money.

No—but she couldn't believe Ty would ever do such a thing, though he would no doubt lock him away and make him into a freak show, charging admission and gathering hefty profit. It was just in his personality to think of money before anything else.

But she had to tell somebody about this strange man in her apartment. About his eyes glowing with such intensity she felt the room could move. She wanted to tell about his touch, and the image of them making love. How it distracted her in such a way the sensational longing for him worked through her like wildfire.

She tried not to believe it, not to think about the ridiculous idea this man was unworldly. Though he'd somehow penetrated her defenses, breaking down her walls to see what was inside her soul. Like digging through a box, he'd found what he needed. She was the one who unleashed him.

She knew he meant no harm. After all, he'd saved her from being robbed or worse yet, killed. He'd plenty of chances to succeed in doing terrible things to her, but he had remained, for the most part, gentlemanly, and she hardly believed he would hurt her now. But still, there was apprehension in his presence.

This story was becoming way too fantastic. Though she'd always been fascinated by ghost stories, she never imagined anything like this would happen to her.

With her breath held, she turned to find him sitting at the table, facing her with a deep stare. There was something in the way he looked, temperate eyes tied into hers—it made her relax. A tingling sensation worked across her skin, and she realized he was trying to enchant her again.

It took every bit of strength to tear from his mesmerizing gaze, but she managed to break free. "Don't ever do that again," she said, completely annoyed he'd invaded her mind. "If you wish to talk with me then talk, but don't do things against my will."

"Forgive me," he said in a soft and sorrowful voice.

"What do you want from me?"

He turned his head and snickered, finding humor in her question. She gave him a stern eye, unable to join him in his brief intermission. And seeing she had no intent on giving in, he straightened his lips and lowered his dark brows.

"I've been waiting for you for many thousands of years, Katherine. As my body waited to be released from my dreaded coffin, my soul drifted alone in darkness." He arched his brows curiously and his eyes gave a hint of color. "I will make you believe it."

She quickly turned away. "I told you to never do that again!" she yelled.

"You demand this, yet you refuse to consider listening to the truth?" he asked, raising his voice as he stood up and walked toward her. "Give me a chance to explain before you condemn me as a liar. Let me show you."

She held out her hand ready to shove him back. "Stay away!"

"You don't wish for me to stay away." He grinned as he stepped inside her boundary and stopped just before her.

He slid his hand over her cheek and through her hair. He grabbed the back of her head and leaned down, and before she could refuse, pressed his lips to hers.

The scent of the sea on his skin wafted into her nostrils, sending her into a state of wonder and vivid fascination. The image of him making love to her invaded her thoughts again, and a passionate sensation coursed through her.

It was pure enchantment as she slid her arms around his neck, caressing him, pressing her body to his. Tears came to her eyes, but it wasn't from fear, it was oddly from sadness.

Images distorted in a mist, but she could see well enough as she slipped into a house built of wood and stone, darkened by the night. And the enclosure held only one other inhabitant, a young man full of terrible remorse—Derrick.

His eyes blazed viciously as he stood over a white horse, crying desperately as it lay dead on the ground. Sobbing as if he'd lost this soul to an unseen evil, he fell to his knees and shouted loudly.

Katherine jumped, startled by his sudden outburst. But her heart sank with deep regret as he leaned his head on the horse's back.

"Forgive me," he whispered. "My Goddess, I have failed you."

She watched as a small group of people surrounded him. Two women dressed in light cloth took hold of his arms and lifted him to his feet. They turned him to face one darkly cloaked man holding a tall twisted wooden staff at his side.

The vision became clear and Katherine could finally make out the scene. With Derrick's right hand covered in blood, he wiped it across his forehead, leaving a dull red mark on his pale skin.

He lifted his chin proudly, showing his stern gaze as he lifted his other hand and showed them the item he held. Gasps came from the small group followed by whispers and moans of pure devastation.

Katherine stared at the article, unsure of what it was. But by the way they acted, it was obviously very important to them.

"You may look closer," Derrick said as he walked through the angry men and crying women, completely unnoticed. "They cannot see us."

"Where are we?" she asked as she took hold of his arm and walked with him.

"We are not in another place but are actually walking through one of my memories, just as I walked through yours."

"So you've invaded my mind again."

"You want to know who I am. There's no better place to begin than the ending."

"What do you mean?" she asked, watching a woman's still frame as she walked around her. It wasn't until she reached Derrick's motionless body did she stop and investigate.

His tears were stuck to his face, frozen, but ever so poetic in heart-wrenching pain. With blood and sweat staining his forehead, his omnipotent stature seemed weak and weary.

"They are Druids, servants to their king. His counsel was evil, a prodigy of religious acolytes and Pagan mystics. He believed in a horse, a Goddess of unlimited power, and coveted her prize possession—a single horn on her head holding within it immortality and magic of the universe. As you can imagine, one with such gifts would embrace the power of the gods, and this terrible king desired it."

Katherine glanced at the smooth white spiraled article in his blood-stained hand. It resembled a horn, but she refused to believe it was from a unicorn.

"He gave his followers an ultimatum: they choose life by doing his bidding, or death if they declined, so they were forced to pull her through a rift in time. They tied her down in the Realm and awaited their Lordship, but they did not know I had followed."

"There's no such thing as immortality and magic. And now you want me to believe in time travel?"

He gave her a perplexed glance. "Magic in this world was indeed real. Though at first difficult to practice, people were taught to use sleight of hand until they were powerful enough to retrieve a source within the earth, the waters, and eventually the heavens. She gave them this gift, for they were good, kind-hearted people, but some became overwhelmed with greed." He sighed as he looked at the horse. "Her name was Koran. She was my friend, and I her ultimate guardian chosen from the great city above the sea—my home to which I would like to return."

"That's quite a tale."

He stood in front of her, a half-grin playing on his lips, but she closed her eyes tight to block him out.

"You can't deny the truth, Katherine."

"I can and I will."

When she opened her eyes, she found herself back in her kitchen. Finding her lips still touching his, she quickly pulled away.

"You don't believe," he said as she leaned against the wall and folded her arms over her chest.

She shook her head, wiping her lips with the back of her hand. "How can I?"

For a moment she thought he'd grow angry. Lowered brows, eyes suddenly gleaming, but he relaxed his face in disappointment.

"I'm sorry," she said when he gave out a sorrowful sigh.

"You are the only one who can help me return home," he said, keeping to his straight-lipped composure, but oddly a tear marked the corner of his eye.

Every bit of him was masculine, making this remarkable tear

running down his cheek ever more serious and terribly attractive. Clearing her throat nervously, she made her way to the table and sat down beside him. She looked him over, trying not to meet his beautiful sad eyes, but she couldn't resist.

"The vision you showed me," she said. "Are they the people who put you in the coffin?"

"Yes," he replied in earnest.

He looked so sincere at that moment, so innocent. She could tell he believed in this, at least by his serious glance, though she'd rather believe it was a game, and right now she wanted to humor him.

"So what are you looking for? This horn?" she asked curiously.

He eyed her carefully. "I'm uncertain what happened to it, but I believe its magic is still here somewhere. My world needs its magic, for without it, it will die. I only hope it is still standing when I return."

"So when you cut it off," she asked, swallowing down a nervous twitch. "You became immortal then, right?"

"Yes," he replied.

"So that's why the Druids stuck you in the coffin. And you've been trapped at the bottom of the sea with flesh-eating fish all this time." Her skin tingled with a chill at the thought, whether she believed the story or not. "It's truly an awful thing to think about."

"I must apologize," he said with a sigh. "I incorporated my pain into you, giving you a sense of what I went through, but it was only to gather your attention to the key."

She rose from the table, trying not to think of the pain he spoke of, but remembered the sensation well. And although she should be terribly angry he'd made her feel it again, she couldn't help but be heartbroken.

She left for the living room, but he followed her. And when his hands caught her shoulders, he turned her around to face him.

"I can ease your sadness," he said, cupping her cheek in his hand.

She shook her head, not wanting to enjoy his touch. "I'm not going to lie and say I don't feel sorry for you, because I do. I honestly think you need help." She thought for a moment longer. "You came into my life just yesterday, and dropped this unbelievable story in my lap expecting me to believe, but I can't dismiss the strange things I've seen. I just don't know what to do or say to you. I don't know what to think."

"Say you will try to believe," he replied. "Help me find my way home."

"And where is your home?"

"The Realm of Life," he said with a grin.

"And where is this Realm of Life?" she asked with a sigh.

He looked at her, seeing the spark in her eye—one she was unable to hide. He stopped just before her, gazing down at her, running his eyes down to her lips, then back to her curious glance.

Her skin rose as he brushed his lips lightly along her cheek to her ear. And when he opened his mouth, he whispered ever-so sensually the best thing she'd heard all night.

"The Realm of Life is Stonehenge."

Chapter Six

Although Katherine had driven to Amesbury many times with Ty, this trip seemed much more interesting. Maybe it was the company she was with, or quite possibly the lush scenery outside as they drove over green hills and through quaint villages and towns. She gathered everything in—the sights, the sounds, and the scent of freshly cut grass. The aroma of the sea emanated off Derrick's skin, giving the eclectic mix an intoxicating summer fragrance.

She pulled over to the side of the road and parked. Her body tingled in giddiness as she realized she was about to see her favorite place in the world.

But Derrick's face was puzzled as he stared at the giant stones in the far-off field with a straight-lipped frown. It made her wonder what he was thinking, and it was apparent it was the complete opposite of her excited reaction.

Before she could say anything, he opened the car door and stepped out. His tall figure moved forward and he began his march toward the circle without her.

Katherine hurried out of the car, locked it, and slipped the keys inside her dress pocket as she fell into stride beside him. The look he gave was astonishingly grim.

"Is something wrong?" she asked, ignoring the fact they were walking in grass instead of the immediate pathway.

"There are stones missing," he muttered, unable to take his eyes off the structure. He stopped abruptly, forcing her to jump ahead slightly before she too stopped.

As they stood amidst the ancient stones, she suddenly lost her breath. "I never seem to tire of their beauty," she whispered.

"This is the entrance to the Forgotten Realm, Katherine," he interrupted. "Five powerful Magi are buried along the boundaries of the circle to create a portal of time."

Katherine couldn't help but snicker at his remark, but she quickly dispersed the humor when she found him frowning in serious discontent. With a clearing of her throat, she watched him pace in the grass, recollecting his memory.

"Here," he said pointing as he marched toward the center of the site. "This stone marks the beginning. The angle should position the next bearing."

She followed him, fully infatuated by his movement as he turned, pointing in one direction, and then found another point with his eyes. It wasn't until he found all the imaginary lines of a pentagon did he stop just before one perfect stone-built doorway.

The sun shone marvelously through it. With golden streams from setting sunlight, it looked as if it were a center on a beautifully painted mural.

"The timing is impeccable," he said, finding a smile. "The beginning and the end are here, Katherine. Do you have it with you?"

"Have what?" she asked finding a chill.

She trembled as he took her by the hand and pulled her against him, and she wondered what was about to happen. Was he going to become a monstrous killer—the bad guy she'd dreaded he'd turn into? Or was he going to hold her, confessing a love ever-lasting?

"I have it now," he said with a grin. "It's been so long since I've seen my home. I've been locked away, unable to return to see my brothers and my friends. It's time I went back on one final walk."

He leaned down and exultantly kissed her lips. And when he broke from their embrace, he stepped back toward the stone doorway.

"Wait. Where are you going?" she asked, confused as to why he was telling her goodbye when there was nowhere to go.

"I promise I will think of you always."

She glanced at his foot as it caught the ground underneath the doorway. The heel of his shoe miraculously disappeared, and she realized he was indeed leaving her. And when she found the diamond in her grasp missing, she wasn't about to let him get away.

Without thinking, she took a quick step and caught him by the arm just as he turned and walked through. He faltered slightly by her sudden weight on him causing her to also lose her balance.

She grabbed tightly to his arm expecting to fall to the ground. Hoping his body would minimize the blow, she huddled against him, shutting her eyes tight.

But the ground never came.

He picked her up into his arms as if rescuing her from a fast flowing wave, threatening to pour over her feet at the beach. At first the sudden movement was disorienting, but when she opened her eyes she caught her stability.

Everything seemed normal as she peered over Derrick's broad shoulder, hanging her arms loosely around his neck. The ancient stones were there, but falling far behind them as he walked forward. She turned her gaze to him, his angry face evident.

"You could have killed us both," he said. "And I would be on the other side by now if you hadn't followed me in."

"Well, if you hadn't stolen my diamond, I wouldn't have followed you!" she exclaimed nervously. She glanced above her. "Where in the world are we?"

Clouds painted crisp blue sky, moving rather quickly as if the winds were strong, fierce with storm. It was breathtaking, but unusual—she couldn't feel any of it whipping around her.

She leaned over, careful not to fall from his arms as she looked down. Far below his feet, the ocean waves rolled with the wind as if it too carried the storm. It was then she realized they were walking on still air.

With wild eyes, she began to struggle to get a better grip on his neck. Fear rose into the back of her throat and found its way to her voice. With a quick thrust of her jaw, she belted out the loudest scream that had ever left her mouth before, sending her into a state of ultimate panic.

"Katherine!" Derrick yelled overtop of her cries, straining his voice from the grip she had around his neck. "Calm down or you'll be the death of both of us!"

"How are we doing this?" she cried. "This is impossible!" She closed her eyes, squeezing tears from the inside corners onto the bridge of her nose. "This is just another dream—a really, really bad dream!"

"Please," he pleaded, interrupting her humming voice as she tried to meditate her nightmare away. "Loosen your hold on me."

"I can't!"

"You must or you'll take my breath! The ocean is far below and I don't wish for us to end our journey together there."

She found the courage to loosen her hold on him, but just enough for him to draw in a deep breath and exhale in relief. Leaving her eyes closed, she began following his direction to breathe with him.

"Relax, Katherine," he said in a deep, soothing voice. "Take a deep breath then let it out slowly. Refrain from opening your eyes."

The tears stopped as she began to think about the impossible situation. His feet seemed rigid enough on whatever he was walking on. His arms held her securely enough. And even in the possible event they'd fall, there was no getting around it, nothing to grab hold of, and definitely no other alternative to the situation. She only had one choice, to loosen her grip and breathe normally. Finally able to get herself under control, she breathed. Panic began to fade, but her nerves were still weary and her body still trembled. But if she kept her eyes closed, maybe she could forget. A conversation was at hand.

"What is this place?" she asked, hoping the answer to his question would ease her mind over the probable long fall to her untimely demise.

"This is empty space," he answered quickly.

"Of course it is," she said cynically, finding the courage to open her eyes to his.

He managed a grin as he turned his gaze forward, continuing his walk with her in his arms.

"Matter is absent in many places in the Universe," he continued. "We have discovered a technology within our magic to produce fractures within certain places, allowing us to walk through time, though we cannot control how far forward or back we can go. And the trip to and from our destination can only be traveled once in our lifetime before the unique tear closes to us forever."

"Are you kidding?" she asked, completely stunned by his absurd answer. "This is an illusion, some visual stunt pulled by Hollywood directors. And you're nothing more than a thieving actor saving the damsel in distress."

"I dare not throw a cover over your eyes and deceive you," he replied, surrendering a dashing grin to her speechless eyes. "I will always tell you the truth, Katherine."

"So did you steal my diamond?" she asked, already knowing the answer to her question.

"Yes," he replied.

"You will return it won't you?"

"I will," he replied, causing her to melt within his unbelievable stare.

As if she'd been privy to them, she suddenly felt his arms around her. Strong but holding her gently, he kept his grasp steady and unyielding. To feel so comfortable in them made her realize she was definitely in some sort of reverie, or quite possibly he was the greatest actor she'd ever met.

"So where are we going?" she asked.

He arched his brows in inexorable excitement. "There," he motioned with a nod for her to turn her attention forward. "I am finally home."

It seemed slow motion as she turned her gaze forward and found an image of a city appearing among the clouds. Golden domes and small arched structures reflecting marvelous sunlight glistened in her eye as he carried her through and stepped down onto the flat capstone of a beautifully constructed pyramid.

He drew in a deep breath as he gently dropped her to her feet, and then let it out noisily, proudly. "Invigorating," he said as he gazed out over his home.

Katherine stood rigid, awe-inspired and breathless in the center of the golden city. Comparable to heaven beside the sea, light bended to create nothing more than a perfect paradise. Too elaborate to be created by some Hollywood studio, and too beautiful to be real, wherever she was, it held no modern place on the globe.

Sounds of harps and beautiful operatic voices singing melodic pleasures rose from the streets and flooded her ears. Her heart began to ache in joyous tension as if the angels themselves created the exquisite music just for her arrival.

"Spectacular," she whispered as she watched the bluest of waters through the stone crevices of the streets, mapping out large intricate shapes of sea-life.

She traced the outer wall of the city with her eyes and found the land hugging the sea. A port of ships with sails as tall as the pyramid she stood on rocked lovingly with the lapping waves. And people lined sandstone walkways littered with markets, chatting lively in friendly manners, laughing with one another as if they hadn't a care in the world.

She arched her brows in fascination. "How is it possible to hear them from so far away?" she asked Derrick, unable to take her eyes away. "And I can see them as if they stood directly in front of me."

"You can see them?" he asked, completely aghast by her observation. "No outsider has ever been able to see through the Eyes."

"The Eyes?" she asked.

"Yes," he replied. "The pyramid we stand on is the Eyes of the city. From here we are able to find what has been lost. We're able to see what lies beyond the boundaries of our city—past, present, and future."

"You can see the future from here?" she asked, her voice breathy in allure to know more.

She inhaled wonderful scents, closing her eyes. A mixture of wild flowers and sea mingled in the wind blowing gentle and warm through her long dark curls. It gave her peace of mind, not only in mysticism, but the fact her feet were on solid ground.

Her eyes suddenly fell on Derrick, his dark hair waving in the wind as if it had taken on a life and, too, was happy to be home. He flashed his strong, unbelievable grin. And just as she became aware of his hand gently palming her face, she felt it slowly slip away as he turned his attention on a large crowd of people running up the steps toward them.

"Do not fear our language when you hear it, for we may sound a tad frightening to an outsider. Our tones are deep, but our hearts are filled with peace. I will translate what is said for you after we settle."

"Brother!" a smiling, and rather handsome man shouted as he came to stand on the step below Derrick, his voice a normal young man's tenor. "It has been too long!"

Derrick quickly took his hand and pulled him into his arms. "You have no idea how long it has been."

They oddly bowed to him as he passed.

Though strong and handsome among these unusual people decorated in blue-beaded necklaces contrasting perfectly in their white chitons, he stood out in his modern day garments. But he acknowledged each one with a nod as if he were a noble, and they his followers.

Katherine glanced down at herself. In her simple little flower print dress with two clumsily stitched front pockets, she felt below a commoner's status, more like a slave girl awaiting her master's order.

With a wave of his hand, Derrick motioned her to follow. And as if she were exactly what she'd just thought, she obeyed his wish. "You've been gone three years. Father did not serve us with answers," the blond man said.

"I'm sure his abhorrence for me has kept him from disclosing my whereabouts." Derrick stopped at the bottom stair and placed his hand on his brother's shoulder. "The horn of Koran was severed. And if three years have passed, it's plenty of time for an army to develop in the north. With their knowledge of the portal, they could easily slip into our city and destroy our way of life."

"No," he said in a cautious whisper only Derrick could hear. He narrowly eyed him. "It is not them we need to fear."

"Katherine," Derrick said. "This is my brother."

"Yes, I know," she said with her attention on the young blond-haired man returning her nervous grin with one of his own.

"You know our language," the man beamed brightly, arching his brow in fascination.

"No," she replied courteously. "But I understand as if you speak mine."

"Incredible," Derrick said. "No outsider has ever deciphered our language before." He shook off his bewilderment and presented his brother with an outstretched hand. "You may call him Mortin."

"Mortin?" she asked with a squint to her eye and a twist of her lips, thinking it an odd name.

Mortin quickly took her by the hand and raised it to his lips. "Mortin it is for you, pretty lady."

"Ah, still the charmer I see," Derrick said as he grasped her hand and pulled it away from his brother.

He held on to her as they continued walking. She watched her feet as she stepped on dark stone, resembling the ones from Stonehenge. A flat surface, chiseled with markings familiar to her felt good beneath her bare feet.

"Stop," she said to Derrick, but caused everyone in the group to halt and turn their attention to her. Realizing she'd just caused a small scene, she curved her lips into a quaint, uneasy frown. "My diamond, if you don't mind."

Derrick glanced down at his hand. "Damn! It must have fallen from my grasp," he said. "Do not worry. There are no thieves here. I will find it as soon as we're settled in my house."

Katherine meant to argue, but Mortin cleared his throat, gathering Derrick's attention. "Uh ..." he stammered. "About your house ..."

"What about my house?" Derrick lowered his brows into a glare. "Did that damned woman take over my abode while I was gone?"

"She couldn't help it. Her husband demanded they live there until you returned."

"Husband?" he shouted angrily. "Damn her!"

Derrick let go of Katherine's hand and stormed off up the street. Nobody followed him, including Mortin who practically duck-and-covered. The worry on his face, prominent and overbearing, was enough to spark her curiosity.

With a quick step she squeezed through the crowd, keeping her eyes on the target as he stormed through the small city. She found herself moving across stones, leaping over streams venturing across the walkway until at last he stopped at a large stone-built house.

Katherine ogled at the landscaping around it. Gorgeous green shrubs were planted around a sculpted fountain. White winged horses stood tall in a small stream filled with multi-colored leaves floating in its bright blue water, giving off a hint it was fall, but it felt as hot as a mild summer day.

As she walked slowly into the small courtyard, astounded by the visuals of her surroundings, she caught sight of something extraordinarily familiar. And her skin rose as she walked toward it, hand over mouth.

Just above the spout, translucent water spewing from the mouth of a five-holed silver metal pipe stood her design. Two arches hung beautifully outside twisted pieces, resembling the white horse from her dream. It was perfectly captured, exactly as she'd imagined, and exactly how she'd designed it to look overtop of his coffin.

Swallowing down anxiety, she returned her attention to Derrick who was now shouting for someone to open the door. He pounded heavily with a clenched fist until the door opened to a rather distressed young woman.

He quickly pulled her out of the house, nearly jerking the poor thing's arm off. She fell to the ground, horror looming in her eyes as if he were a ghost returning from the grave to haunt her.

"I'm so sorry," she pleaded. "I could not wait for you any longer."

Katherine thought daggers would shoot from his eyes. The woman was obviously his love interest when he was here. It had to hurt him to know she'd found someone else while he spent thousands of years in torment.

"Get out of my house!" Derrick demanded as a nice looking blonde man ran to her side and pulled her from the ground to her feet.

Katherine watched as two beautiful young children, twins with long brown hair ran to their mother's side, crying with worry. It broke her heart to see such a display of hostility happen before them, but she could see the sudden distressed disposition in Derrick's eyes.

"Forgive me," he said as he let out a deep overwrought sigh. "I didn't know."

Katherine watched him walk away. Without a glance back, he ventured out onto the street. The crowd of people gathering outside the courtyard fence offered their condolences, but he didn't acknowledge them as he turned his way up the road.

As the people went about their business, she walked out onto the street. Eyeing his back, he walked despondently toward a large golden-domed building resembling what could be the city's capitol.

She followed, unsure of whether to catch up to him or not. Thinking he didn't really need cheering, or there was no possible way to liven up someone who'd lost a loved one to another in his absence, she strayed behind.

As she walked she heard whispers of his return, some fearing thoughts of his father's mood over him bringing in an outsider. Though his brother showed no ill will against meeting her, the eyes watching were very worried.

Realizing she had no idea where in the world, or out of the world, she was, she decided to catch up to him. Quickening her pace, she found herself falling into stride beside him as they entered the domed building.

"I know you're upset over finding your love lost to someone else," she said, hoping her choice of words weren't out of place. "But could you please tell me where we are?"

He walked solemnly across white stone partially painted in teal and black checkers. She followed until she found herself gazing at the ceiling with incredible wonder.

"Zeus, Hades, Poseidon," she whispered. "These illustrations are fantastic. I've never seen such a display. Well, except for Michelangelo's Genesis in the Sistine Chapel."

She traced the images with her eyes. A loving display of blended paint into stone captured the God of the sky in poetic white as if he'd been drawn in the clouds themselves. Blue sky rapture seemed to hold his being steady as he reined over the lobby where she stood.

Hades, black as the night with eyes red as wine, stared at her viciously, mesmerizing her into overexcitement as if she were actually seeing him in truth for the very first time. His hand outstretched, as he led a woman into the underworld.

Poseidon was placed in dead center as if he ruled over this abode. A strange position considering Zeus was much more powerful than he was. Water flowed from his eyes, peculiarly painted turquoise as if resembling the same glow she'd seen from Derrick's eyes.

She searched the room and found Derrick on a large stone chair at the top of a short flight of stairs, sitting chin to fist—sulking. The frown he wore deepened his appearance, and it lured her to him.

"I know you're upset," she said as she knelt down in front of him, placing her hand on his knee. "I've gone through heartbreak before and it's never easy. But in time you'll learn to push it to the back of your mind and hopefully forget."

He sighed. It wasn't so much an aggravated groan, but more of disappointment, possibly taking heed life went on without him.

"I wish I knew what to tell you," she continued. "I'm sure you loved her."

"It's not because she married another man," he finally spoke up. "It's the fact she kept my house. What of my belongings? And how did she find permission from my father of all things?"

"Your father?" she asked, amused at the fact he wasn't upset over the love of the woman, but more of his things.

He glanced at the ceiling and arched a brow in perplexed exasperation. "The fool can't keep his hands to himself," he said impatiently, propping himself up. "Did you see the children? They were the spitting image of him."

"I don't understand," Katherine answered, watching as he glared at the ceiling.

"Do you hear me father?" he yelled, causing a mighty echo in the round vestibule. "Did you rape her or did you give her an ultimatum? Every damn woman I find interest in, he has to take them from me! Why do you hate me so much?"

Katherine looked around, waiting for someone to answer, but he was clearly talking to the painting on the ceiling. Possibly he'd found it easy to use the image as a way to communicate with his father who was actually deceased? She shrugged.

"My father," he huffed out an aggravated groan as he stood on his feet. "He is a worthless god who does not deserve a human soul. He woos innocent young women to his bed, fathering children who end up in this abysmal hell of a city. I should have stayed away." He gazed back at the ceiling. "Do you hear me? You're a worthless god and a pitiful excuse for a father!"

Katherine felt the floor begin to shake. At first she thought she'd gone weak in the knees since she hadn't a morsel to eat all day. But when the tremor grew to a violent quake, she began to panic.

"Come on," Derrick said as he grabbed her arm and jerked her to her feet.

They ran, stumbling until they found their way outside and threw themselves to the ground just in time to watch the giant dome fall before them.

With Derrick's crushing weight overtop of her, she covered her ears, muffling the thunderous noise of heavy stone crashing down to the ground. She coughed as dust flew into her face, stinging her eyes with gold sediment and white sandstone.

"Unbelievable!" Derrick shouted to the heavens as he stood up on his feet, staggering as if he'd had too much to drink. Ignoring the few pebbles still rolling from the colossal ruined mess, he shouted again.

"Who are you yelling at?" Katherine screamed as she wiped dusty tears from her eyes.

She sat on her rear and eyed her dress. The front was torn, frayed to her mid-thigh exposing skinned knees. She pulled dust and pebbles into her hands, and like a child throwing a tantrum, threw it out into the settling air.

"Oh now," he said as he knelt down before her and thumbed the dust from her wet face. "Don't cry. The building will be good as new by evening."

"I don't care," she said, her voice whiny and ultimately cross. "I just want to end this nightmare and go home."

He chuckled. "Look now," he continued. "Your knees are bleeding. Come with me to my other house and I'll treat your wounds." He stood up tall and held out his hand for her once more.

She glanced up as he shielded the sun from her eyes with his magnificent form. His long dark hair waved in the breeze giving off the impression he was proud and somewhat cocky.

Right now she couldn't stand him, thinking him making fun of her as she cried. But she had no choice but to swallow her tears and go with him.

She accepted his proposal and took his hand. As he pulled her to him she noticed a group of cloaked individuals walking ominously up the pathway toward the broken building. Hooded in radiant white, they looked heavenly, like angels.

As Derrick guided her down the walkway, she turned her head and looked back. She watched as the group separated, encircling the stone rubble. They raised their arms over their heads, and a hymn found her ears, beautiful, enchanting, and downright eerie.

She gasped remembering what Derrick had told her just moments after the building fell. As the chants grew louder, the broken structure began to pull back together causing the air to glitter once again with gold. No tools, no heavy machinery, just magic reconstructing it pebble by pebble, and stone by stone.

"Pretty neat huh?" Derrick said, grinning as he watched her astounded reaction. "Our Magi are powerful here, the most powerful in the universe."

As they turned the street corner taking them out of view, she returned her attention to him. She brushed her face with her hands, wiping off as much sand and tears as she could.

"Exactly where are we?"

"We are in Atlantis," he answered proudly, grinning at her as he opened the door on a petite but rather charming house at the end of the street. It was cottage-like, but landscaped just as beautiful as his last already engaged home.

"Atlantis?" she repeated the word and squeezed a few more tears from her eyes. "I shouldn't be surprised," she mumbled. "Everything else about this dream has been off the wall."

"So which one is your father?" she asked, feeling a little more reassured by her decision to let her dream work out on its own.

"Poseidon," he answered as he pulled her inside the house and breathed a sigh, thankful it was empty.

"Wait," she said, stopping just before a large square stone tub of water on a pedestal in the center of the room, bubbling and steaming as if it had been waiting on her. "Are you saying you're the son of Poseidon, the God of the Sea, the ruler of horses, and one of the biggest womanizers in Greek mythology?"

"Yes," he replied, obviously taken back by her knowledge of him and the fact she'd spoken in such a cynical tone. "How do you know so much?"

"I took a small course in mythology."

"You use the word freely," he said, fascinated by her words. "We are real here in Atlantis." He glanced upward then returned his gaze to her. "The gods are true, not legends and tales told by scholars. And I am here, with you, not a figment of story or dream."

"Stay away," she said as he made his way toward her. She stepped back from his dawdling chase. "I admit I've never dreamt so vividly before, but there is no other explanation to this madness."

She found herself pinned against the wall. He stopped just before her and touched her face with the back of his hand. Swallowing hard, she found the strength to turn away, but in the wrong direction as her eyes caught his luxurious bed.

Dressed in lovely red silk, it was turned down as if waiting her arrival. White satin sheer draped across the top of the posts and hung daintily overtop creating a see-through marquee. It was way too quixotic for such a dirt-covered woman.

"I really need to wash this sand off," she said with a slight whisper, returning her gaze to his.

He palmed her cheek and grinned, showing his magnificent white teeth and arching his shaded brows with intent. She thought he could pass as a prince for sure, a dark lord with ulterior motives to whisk her into bed with him.

Yes, she thought arduously, she'd play along with this dream. There was no way he was the son of Poseidon, but more likely, son of Hades. He had the look down superbly. He'd only told her the tale so she wouldn't be scared of his nature—and that was as true heir to the Underworld.

"The spring is there," he said, motioning briefly at the tub with his eyes. "It is warm and ready for you whenever you like."

"Strange," she whispered, trying to ignore the proximity of his face, his lips near hers. "I must be dreaming."

"Is it too convenient?" he asked as if reading her mind.

"Honestly yes," she replied. "But I'll play along."

Weakness suddenly hit her knees. She'd fought the attraction to him for so long, but her heart inadvertently pounded in her chest. His body held her still with just a brush of his chest against hers, and his lips touched her sandy tear-stained cheek.

He leaned next to her, hands against the wall above her head. And when she felt his breath on her ear, she trembled.

She leaned back expecting him to continue, hoping he'd move his lips to hers, but he refrained. Instead he smiled.

"If this is just a dream, Katherine," he said his voice soothing in her ear. "Then why do you tremble when I'm near?" With a short sigh, he stood straight, releasing her from his hold. "I'll leave you to your bath."

She watched him walk away. As he trudged toward the door, the thought of letting him out of her sight weighed heavily on her heart, on the state of arousal he'd put her in.

"Wait," she called after him as he left the premises.

He stopped and turned around, a grin returning to his face. "Take this alone time to bathe. There are clothes for you to wear in the armoire beside the bed."

"Where are you going?" she asked.

"The market is just down the street. I'll be back with something for us to eat."

She shivered as she watched him leave, and fear of being left alone in this strange place worked her nerves. But when she turned, she swallowed down her apprehension and made her way to the armoire.

A large old-wood wardrobe stood before her, a rather eerie looking thing with its black knots and crooked cut structure. It definitely wasn't built by carpenter hands. She almost dreaded opening it as she took hold of the imperfect brass handles, held her breath, and then pulled open the double doors to reveal an incredible display of colors.

She arched her brow in fascination and a smile broke on her lips. It lingered as she began searching through an extravagant selection of modern dresses and old chitons.

She pulled out a light blue, long sleeve linen dress woven in silver thread. The garment would be perfect for a cool day, but it was terribly hot outside. She hung it back inside, eyeing it one more time before she moved to the next dress.

She pulled out a peach linen gown, long in length but thin. Laying it on the bed, she admired the loose silver stitching along the straight cut neckline and two simple shoulder straps. It was very modern for something supposed to be of ancient Greece, but who was she to argue with her dream.

If her dream ended before she was able to feel it against her skin, she was going to be livid. And although the thought of wearing it was exciting, she couldn't help but wonder where it came from and who it belonged to.

She quickly undressed. Sand and pebbles scattered across the stone floor creating short spurts of clatter. The sound raised her spirits in a humorous way, and she wondered how in the world that much rubble could fit inside one simple dress.

She tittered as she piled her clothes on the floor beside the tub and walked up the sandstone steps. With a quick dip of her toes, she tested the temperature of the water—perfect.

As she lowered herself into the tub, covering herself to her neck in its warmth, she wondered how it was possible. Obviously there was a lack of knowledge for electricity with all the candles burning around the room. But of course electricity hadn't been discovered yet, at least she gathered this.

She chortled again at her thoughts, closed her eyes and gave out a sigh. The bath was soothing with an allusion of lavender, possibly soap, that was dissolved earlier. But she paid no mind to it as she tried to relax and ignore the deep growl coming from the pit of her stomach. And if Derrick didn't get back soon with something for her to eat, she was going to break down again, and deliberately cry.

Chapter Seven

Rosemary. The scent lingered through the window as Katherine tied her dark curls loosely on the back of her head with a white gem-studded comb. Her stomach growled in a horrible way.

She wished she could see what she looked like, but not a mirror could be found in the small dwelling. The only reflection she could find was from the water in the tub that had strangely stopped bubbling as if it were on some sort of timer.

She thought it odd with all the antiquities around her, there was a taste of modern ability. The candles, although lit beautifully around the room, burned sandalwood scented oil, and seemed an endless supply. And she thought it peculiar that every time she moved, they followed her, lighting her way around the small stone house. And if she hadn't been dreaming, she would have already brought one down and inspected it.

But now the Rosemary scent masked the room, and her stomach rumbled as she caught the scent mingling with that of fish grilling outside. She touched the brass handle of the door, recognizing the amateur handy-work to be the same design as the wardrobe. With a hesitant pull, she opened it and walked outside.

Her heart leapt at the sight of him standing in front of a stone-built grill, cooking fish on a slab of clay. The low burning fire seemed to meld in his eyes, giving a yellowish tint within the unusual sea blue—beautiful.

His hair glistened wet, tied back to show off his pale chiseled face matching his thin white shirt. She thought it odd he wore a pair of dark pants and light slip-on sandals, making him look more like a modern man relaxing on the beach, rather than someone from an ancient legendary world.

It was just like her to dream up a man like him—sexy, confident.

And though son of a Greek god, she believed he deserved to be one as well—the god of temptation.

With a slight clearing of her throat, she walked toward him, gathering his attention. A strange insecure look took over the cockiness he'd presented before as he watched her approach. His eyes widened, and in a clumsy moment, the wooden utensil fell from his hand and dropped to the ground at his feet.

The way he looked at her, taking in the way the peach dress hugged her curves, made her feel beautiful. But after his eyes wandered over her once, he returned his attention to the sizzling fish in front of him.

"You look stunning Katherine," he said as he picked up the utensil from the ground and wiped it with a white cloth on the edge of the grill. "But you should take the garment from your shoulders."

Katherine glanced down at the simple white frock. Agreeing it looked a tad trite, she carefully pulled it over her head. She draped it over the large stone block beside the grill and sat down on it.

"You didn't find any shoes?" he asked as he began to flake the fish.

"Yes," she replied. "But the warm stone feels good on my bare feet."

He grinned as he picked up the slab. Breathing in the scent, he set it down on the stone beside her. He turned and sat facing her as he hungrily picked up a large hunk of meat between his fingers and stuck it in his mouth.

She knew as hungry as she was, she could probably do the same, but she remained proper and pulled a small pinch. He watched her as she stuck it in her mouth and daintily chewed.

"I know you are a lady," he said, swallowing his bite. "But I also know how hungry you are. Don't worry about being prim around me. I'll not poke fun."

"It's very good," she said, ignoring his advice.

"I almost forgot," he said, quickly standing to his feet.

He strode to the front gate and picked up a large oval basket. With a strong grin, he made his way back to his seat and happily presented it to her.

"The woman who owns the market I frequent said I should offer you more than fish for dinner. I myself can live on meat alone, but a woman needs sweet fruits and scones." He gazed into the basket. "I believe she added a spoon of honey in there as well."

She watched him search the basket. A measure of cuteness fell over him, giving him the appearance of a small boy in a candy store.

A meat eater indeed, she thought as he pulled out a perfect golden pear and studied it. With a lively perk to his grin, he opened his mouth and bit into it.

"This is good," he said glancing at her as if he'd suddenly found heaven. "If you think about it," he continued as he chewed, "I haven't eaten in thousands of years." The sudden curiousness in his face showed as he gazed upward, thinking. "I wonder how I'm not completely insane."

Katherine pulled out a bunch of large red grapes, perfectly ripened and still on the vine. She picked one off and popped it in her mouth, tossing Derrick a curious glance.

"Were you aware of yourself inside the coffin? I mean, while your body was eaten away, were you able to feel pain?"

His face suddenly fell flat and pale. He leaned his forearm across his lap, fumbling the half-eaten pear in his hand as he stared at it.

"I'm sorry," she said, feeling rather awkward for bringing up an obvious sore subject.

"No," he said, giving her a reassured grin. "No need to apologize. It's just very difficult to explain."

"Can you try?"

He gave her a short nod. "There is a university, just through the forest beyond the wall and overlooking the sea. I spent many days learning the ways of the world. Scholars are hand-picked from our fathers to teach magic, engineering, construction, and just within the past hundred years, the ability to open up empty space."

"Time travel," she recalled.

"Yes," he replied. "From the Eyes, scholars were able to see the potential to spread our knowledge to the world outside. We wanted to learn more about them and their ways of life, and in return, they wanted to learn our magic. Our first contact was the Druids."

"They were peaceful according to history."

"We all carry demons, Katherine. Some just show themselves a little more than others. When we introduced our magic to them, they were hospitable and kind. They were able to learn quickly because of the ease to work with them. At first we were pleased, but their greed began to show. They wanted more than what we were offering, and our gods allowed them to have all they wanted. Few became so dominant they began tapping into heaven's power, and then they captured my goddess."

"See," she said, watching as he began picking through the fish again. "I just have a hard time believing any of this. If these gods are truly real, how come I've never seen or heard them?"

"I'll take you to the western sea someday. We'll tour the University so you'll see our ways."

A moment went by in silence. The only sound came from the fire crackling inside the grill and the ocean crashing on the rocks in the distance.

She took the opportunity to concentrate on filling her stomach, not knowing when the next meal would be. As she ate, questions rolled around inside her, and she found it excruciating he hadn't answered the only one she'd asked him.

The fact he'd blamed her for calling him a liar was fueling another fire within her. And maybe it was the agitated look she held making him touch her arm lightly, gathering her attention.

"I didn't mean to upset you," he said as he slid his hand to hers and held it gently. "The answers you seek are difficult and can only be made known by demonstration. I swear you'll not leave my city without answers."

"I just want to know how it's possible. How many years were you inside it? How are you here, alive and in front of me if it's been thousands of years?" She stood up, rather annoyed.

She began to pace, glancing up into the perfect night sky. Not a cloud was showing amongst the bright stars flickering sporadically, casting diverse pastels around each one.

"See what I mean?" she stuck her finger up, pointing at the unusual pattern of light. "This is not normal. This is not how the sky looks from my house." She paced again, breathing deeply, pinching herself, jumping up and down, and doing anything she could to wake herself up. "I must be in a coma at a hospital somewhere in London." She suddenly stopped and grinned. "That's it! That's the reason why I can't wake up. Maybe the man's knife hit my back a little more than I thought."

"Katherine," Derrick pleaded as he came to stand before her.

"What can I do to make you believe?"

She frowned, ignoring him but looking straight into his eyes. "Or maybe I'm actually dead."

Her hand covered her mouth, thinking about the extreme possibility. Here she was with the perfect man, in a perfect city, and under a glorious heaven. Quite possibly she could be in Limbo awaiting the Ferryman to guide her across the River Styx—uncanny.

"I'm dead aren't I?"

"You are not dead." He chuckled, giving her a sweet smile. "And you are not in a coma," he added as he thumbed a tear from her cheek. "You are here, with me."

"But I don't belong here," she said.

"Listen," he said pulling her into his arms. "Give it a few days. I'll send you back through as soon as the portal to the Realm reopens."

Though she agreed, she couldn't help but wish her dream would end. She'd wake up in her bed, in her petite apartment in London, and get ready for work.

"I realize you're overwhelmed, but I swear you are safe here. I won't let any harm come to you. I give you my solemn vow."

"I don't have any choice now, do I? I'm a prisoner here, I'm your prisoner!"

Derrick suddenly pulled away from her. He stood up proud, but irritation combined his gaze as he looked down at her, folding his arms over his chest.

"You're such a child," he said. "In all your travels, I'd figured you to be more adventurous. After all, isn't this what archaeologists do?"

"I'm an architect actually, and I'm quite adventurous when the journey is factual. But this place," she looked around her. "This is nothing more than my imagination. And other than the few unexplainable things I've seen, it's not exactly magical."

"Wow," he said appalled by her cynical tone. "Your mood turns on a whim. Unbelievable."

He shook his head in disappointment and quickly turned away. He made his way out of the small courtyard, finding the street.

She watched as a candle hovering at the gate began to follow him. Strangely the flame took on the shape of an orb, just like the one she'd found in the dirt beside the coffin, but newer. Its light grew into a bright shade of red as if it emanated his anger. That was definitely magical.

She suddenly felt bad for making him angry. And she definitely didn't mean for him to leave her there, alone. She stood to her feet and moved toward the gate just as the red flame disappeared around the corner.

"Derrick!" she yelled, finding her feet treading fast over stone. She rounded the corner expecting to find him walking down an empty street, but she came to a sudden halt. She drew in a deep breath as she stared at the incredible sight before her.

Orbs were scattered in the air along the street, floating over many people. The round lights followed them as they danced to music, or just hovered as some stood and talked about their day.

People searched through the open street market, looking through clothing or finding jewelry to try on and buy. Others, smiling richly, browsed through fresh seafood and produce lined on the other side of the street.

Shoppers oohed and aahed at the plentiful selection. And as Katherine began walking toward them, she had the desire to do the same.

She fell into the waltz of the crowd, and a smile dressed her lips as she began to feel quite comfortable. It was the first time she didn't feel out of the ordinary, even with the strangely lit orbs floating around by themselves.

"Try a sample?" A young, blond man with a striking physique offered her a cup of red wine. Wearing nothing but a brown kilt and a blue feathered belt, he grinned proudly. He definitely didn't look like an ancient soul, but more a Celtic enthusiast with the face of an angel.

"Thank you," she said, graciously accepting the large silver cup. A vision of Oktoberfest invaded her mind as she walked further down the street, sipping on one of the best wines she'd ever tasted. People danced to the sounds of bagpipes near the seas port, dressed in the same Celtic clothing.

It wasn't exactly the sound of harps and angelic voices like she'd heard before, but it was without a doubt tuned for a party—and quite a party they were having.

The city of Atlantis wasn't exactly the vision she'd concocted from her studies of lore. Sure it was a city of gold with an obvious link to legend. And indeed it was probably in the spot on the map most believers swore it to be—the image of the shark she'd seen from the pyramid was proof enough.

As she walked onto the wooden sea port, she gazed at the sails towering over her. No other words could describe it, but amazing and breathtaking. And the words "out of the ordinary" came when she saw a dozen or more orbs zipping around rope and net as if playing a game of tag.

She shivered slightly as a cool breeze propelled her hair and danced on her skin, just as she turned and spotted his dark figure sitting on a crate at the edge of the pier. She couldn't see him though his back was turned, but by the fading red glow of the suspended orb over his shoulder, she knew exactly who it was.

With a relieved sigh, she made her way up behind him. She set the cup down on the crate and hesitantly touched his shoulder. She leaned in close to his ear and spoke over the eerie creaking roll of the ships. "I'm sorry."

He turned his attention to her. At first his eyes startled her, a tint of red from the orb showed in them. But when he smiled, it quickly diminished into the darkness of the pier.

"I'm the one who should apologize," he said. "I accused you of acting like a child when it was I who ran away."

"I pushed you into it." She reminded him as she slid up onto the crate, and tucked her arm under his.

He was warm and she didn't deny it felt wonderful on her bare skin. She pulled the cup over with her other hand and indulged in another sip.

"Is this drink the wine from the shop below the fish market?" he asked curiously.

Katherine nodded with a smile. "Would you like a sip?"

"Oh no," he said with a chuckle. "I'll not let his drink pass my lips again."

She swallowed nervously. "Why not?"

"It's very potent." He eyed her peculiarly. "How much have you drank?"

"Only a few sips."

"You'll sleep well tonight then."

"Lovely," she said letting out a worried sigh as she set the cup back down again.

"Unless he's changed the magic in the formula, which I doubt, it won't hit you until you've retired to your bed for the night."

She gave out a short laugh through her nose. "Now that's something you don't hear everyday." She bumped up against him.

"Just beyond the horizon lies a reef. I'll take you to meet the Siren. I haven't seen her since I was a child. She's a rather wicked maiden, frightening to look upon, but I am almost certain she'll help us find your diamond."

"A Siren?" she asked with an inquiring grin.

"Her name is Mila." He hopped off the crate. "Will you believe me if I take you to see her?"

This place was just too fictitious to believe, but she wasn't about to tell him this. Instead she nodded giving him an agreement, for it wasn't worth arguing over any longer.

He held out his hand. "Let's go back to the house."

She slid her palm on his, and with a quick gentle pull, he helped her down from the crate. She landed in his arms at what seemed perfect timing as soft, beautiful music began to play.

"It's lovely," she whispered, sliding her arms around his neck and gazing upward into his eyes as the sound of harps touched her ears in melodic splendor. "I've never heard anything like this before."

"The music is for you then," he whispered his return, grazing her ear with his lips.

"Dance with me," she said, not knowing if it was the drink, or an acceptance to surrender to him. No matter what it was, she knew only one thing—she was beginning to enjoy herself.

He led her with his gentle touch, switching hands as they walked around each other slowly—a dance of the eyes. They held their stare, gazing deeply, heated attraction radiating off their bodies.

"I've never danced with a woman before," he confessed. "Not like this anyway."

"Seriously now?" she said, surprised by his assertion. "I would have believed you to be a ladies man."

"Not quite," he replied as they drew close, clasping hands.

He leaned his forehead on hers, eyeing her intently. The proximity of his lips was perfect, too perfect and undeniably tempting. He pulled her hand upward, draping her arm around his neck and sliding his around her waist. They barely danced with their feet, but passion was moving restlessly in their eyes.

"Kiss me," she whispered, attempting to lure him with a brush of her lips against his.

She closed her eyes, expecting to be taken away in his arms, swept up and deeply embraced, but she felt him pull away. And the cool breeze off the sea caught her breath.

"What's wrong?" she asked, placing her eyes on his unmistakable empty stare. "I guess I should have known better."

She lifted the edge of her dress off her heels and quickly left the pier. Ignoring Derrick's demand for her to wait, she made her way up the street, pushing through the crowd.

She should have known better than to let herself get close. A handsome guy like this was always in her sight, but never in her arms, which was just fine in this case since he was nothing more than a figment of her imagination.

He grabbed her arm just as she walked through the gate to the courtyard. "Katherine!" he insisted. "Let me explain."

"What is there to explain?" she asked, trying not to show how agitated she really was, though she knew he could see right through her. "I made a fool out of myself thinking you were interested."

He shook his head. "You are wrong to feel the fool."

"Then tell me why," she demanded, letting the bottom of her dress fall back around her ankles.

"I—," he stammered. "Want to kiss you more than anything, but..." He let go of her arm and straightened his stance. "How can I show you sincerity, when you don't believe in me?" He arched his brow, completely captivated by his own speech. "And furthermore, if you don't believe in me, then a kiss would mean nothing to you."

She turned on her heel with quarrelling eyes. "But it's just a simple kiss I asked for."

With nose in the air, she made her way to the door, ignoring him as he followed her inside. She tried desperately to get away, but he caught her by the arm and swung her back around to face him.

"You are right," he said as he pulled her hard against him. "It would be just a kiss, and nothing more." He held tight to her arms as she struggled, but he was too strong.

"Unhand me," she said, fighting to break loose from his grasp, but he wouldn't let her go as he quickly leaned down and forcefully pressed his lips to hers.

At first she struggled, fighting him with tightened lips, refusing to let him win. But the weakening of her strength tied with the relentless push of his tongue, softening her lips, her body, and her will.

He loosened the grip on her arms and massaged them sensually. His touch was warm against her rising skin, squeezing gently as he guided her toward the bed.

A kiss and nothing more, she thought as she pulled his shirt over his head knowing she was about to make love to this perfect being, this fictitious man that held her complete attention, and could possibly hold the key to her heart.

She lay back on the bed, watching him climb in overtop of her. The anticipation was strong, but oddly began to diminish as soon as her head hit the pillow. Her eyes suddenly drooped and a drowsy sensation spoiled the arousal, the hunger for his touch.

The last thing she saw before she fell into a deep sleep was Derrick hovering over her with a disappointed look on his face. And the last words he muttered lingered softly in her ears, "Damn that fool's magical drink."

Chapter Eight

A single rose lay on the pillow next to Katherine's head, beautifully open in bloom. Its shade of red seemed to blush in the morning light spectacularly shining through the open windows of the house.

Yawning, she stretched to an awakened state, picking up the rose as she sat. She grinned, bringing it to her nose, and then breathed in its lovely scent.

It had been awhile since she'd received a gift, even one as small and sweet as this. And as she peered through the silky net, she tried to spot the man who left it for her, but he was nowhere to be found.

She slid out of bed and tread to the window, carrying the rose with her. The sun shone beautifully over the flower garden surrounding the fountain. She thought it pleasant to see the display in daylight, and she was suddenly reminded of Derrick's promise to take her out on his ship.

With a skip in her step, she made her way to the armoire and threw the doors open. Since the wind blew cool on the sea, she knew exactly which outfit she was going to wear.

She pulled the light blue dress off the wooden hook and held it before her with a grin. The silver along the neckline seemed polished, perfectly glittering in the light of day.

She positioned it carefully on the bed thinking it the loveliest thing she'd ever seen, though not quite in the fashion of ancient Greek. It was definitely a modern article, new with simple fabric and stitch, but obviously worked on with loving hands. Thin blue see-through silk lined the sleeves, beautifully covering slender shoulder straps.

She quickly disrobed, finding it refreshing to part with the peach dress and indulge in something new. She picked the garment up off her feet and draped it over the post of the bed. But as she did, a cool breeze caught her bare skin.

She covered her breasts with her arm and quickly turned around expecting to see somebody standing there, but she was alone. She shivered as an eerie sensation crept up her spine, as if someone watched her from the shadows, but there was only light in the room.

"Derrick?" she said nervously, glancing around, but his voice didn't return her call.

The tub suddenly began to gurgle, startling her. Steam began to rise from the water dispersing into the air a strange flowery fragrance throughout the room. The fragrance instantly wafted into her nostrils, causing a somewhat leisurely reaction. She breathed a relaxing sigh and walked toward it as if it beckoned her and she had no choice but to obey.

She heard Derrick's voice in her ears, but for some reason she didn't care. All she wanted to do was get in the warm tub and relax, to feel the bubbles caressing her skin. The thought of it excited her, aroused her in a way she couldn't deny. But his voice brought her out of her mesmerized state, just at the brink of the tub. Arms to her side, she turned to face him with a puzzled glance.

"What am I doing?" she asked quickly covering herself with her arms, and blushing profusely over the situation.

He arched his brow, but his eyes were on hers. "Did you not hear me?"

"No," she said, shaking her head as she backed away toward the bed. She quickly retrieved the dress and covered herself, motioning for him to turn away.

He grinned and did as she asked. "I want to apologize for last night," he said peering around the room as if looking for someone who shouldn't be there. "If I had known you were going to follow me, I would have warned you about Lauren's drink."

"No," she said as she slipped her arms through the soft sleeves of the dress and pulled it over her head. "I'm glad he gave it to me. It would be a big mistake to surrender to you."

He turned his head sideways. She could see the arguing glance he gave her as she straightened the garment from her hips to her ankles.

It was a snug fit, but the material stretched slightly, conforming to her figure. She smiled diligently at him as he turned around to face her.

"When are we leaving?" she asked, changing the subject and trying to ignore the fact she'd been lured blindly to the tub. "I'm very adamant about sailing, but I'm willing to be adventurous today."

He couldn't help but return her sentiment. The grin escaping his lips told her how impressed he truly was. Of course it was possible by his wandering eyes he was still envisioning her with nothing on but her bright yellow underwear.

"If you can handle the time warp, you can handle the high seas."

He raised his hand to her face and palmed her cheek. But when she saw him lean, threatening her with a kiss, she quickly pulled away.

"What are we waiting for?" she asked as she walked to the door with a skip in her step. She made her way out into the courtyard and waited on him, knowing her refusal to kiss him belittled his ego.

"Fine," he said as he shut the door behind him and walked out. "Then let's go."

He walked past her without a glance. With a frown and a reddened face, he had all the attributes of aggravation. And though she knew how irritated he was with her, she followed him, generously smiling.

The ships were magnificent in the morning light. As she walked onto the pier, she stared up into the sky, awing at the masts, the tallest as high as a five story building. Her eyes traced the line back down to the pier where Derrick stood watching her intently.

"My ship is at the end of the pier," he said, waving her along as he started walking again.

She watched his back as she followed. The simple clothes he wore made him look like a pirate. His black hair hung down past his broad muscular shoulders to his mid-back, accenting the loose white long sleeve shirt he wore over his black pants that were filled out nicely. A pair of matching boots extended to his mid-calf, and the only thing he was missing was an eye-patch.

He was definitely a bandit, if not only for taking her gem, then at least by stealing her breath, for he was ever so striking to look at. She couldn't help but be terribly attracted to him with her eyes watching his every move, at least until he presented his small, scary looking ship.

He walked up the ramp proudly and excitedly jumped down to the stern. As if the ship had been lost and finally found, he gripped the large wooden helm in his hands and happily squeezed.

"Pegasus," he whispered. "You and I have been apart far too long."

Katherine stood atop the ramp and observed the small ship. Rotted and warped wood abundantly showed throughout the deck and up along the starboard side. The port side wasn't any better, if not worse.

"Come on," he said as he held his hand out to her. "It has blemishes, but I promise we're perfectly safe."

"Blemishes?" she repeated cynically as she hesitantly accepted his hand.

He helped her down into the ship. When her feet hit the wood, it eerily creaked. And the sandals she wore slightly stuck to the floor as she followed him to the helm, creating a sound that would make a maid run away from the work entailed in cleaning it.

"Where's your crew?" she asked, watching him as he started hoisting the anchor.

She nearly lost her footing when the back of the ship leaned, creaking and cracking at the sudden weight of the anchor. She let out a short scream as she fell backward, conveniently falling onto a wooden bench seat just behind the helm.

With her heart in her throat, she held on to the edge until the ship slowed its roll and Derrick returned to the helm. He grinned widely, enjoying the uneasiness on her face.

"Stand up," he demanded, taking her by the hand and pulling her to her feet before she could refuse. He positioned her behind the wheel and quickly placed her hands on it. "Hold on to this while I release the sails. When I call out, I want you to turn it to the left fast and as far as it will go."

"What?" she asked nervously, gripping it tight when he left for the mast. "I don't know how to steer this thing!"

He laughed sharply. "Just listen for my call."

Annoyed he'd found humor in her ignorance, she didn't have

time to bask in it and cause a scene, for he'd already untied the rope around the pole and released the front sails.

The wind whipped it slightly and the ship began to drift slowly forward. A loud scraping sound came from the side as it sideswiped the pier. She cringed, hoping it wouldn't tear out all the loose, rotten pieces and lead them to sink.

"Turn the wheel now!" he shouted as he released the back sails and tied the rope down securely.

"Which way?"

"The left, Katherine, and hurry before we drag the bottom!"

She quickly turned the wheel and the ship began to turn, but she could feel it start to drag. She leaned over and peered as far to the side as she could, trying to get a glimpse of what they were dragging on. The water was deep and there was nothing there she could see.

Derrick dropped down from the rear mast and hurried to the helm, pushing her back. She fell down hard on the bench, glaring at him for his impatience and rough gesture to move her out of his way.

He turned the wheel fast and hard to the left, sending the ship into a severely sharp turn. She watched as the wind caught the sails with a hefty puff, and in no time they came off the sandy bar and were finally heading out to sea.

"Apparently I didn't turn hard enough," she said with a scowl. "Maybe now you'll learn not to force people into doing something they don't want to do."

"You did fine, Katherine," he said as he watched the sails and eyed the ropes to make sure they weren't coming loose. "Maybe next time you won't lead me to believe it's what you want."

"I don't appreciate your tone," she announced proudly, standing to her feet, trying to keep her balance as the ship rose and fell with the waves. "Just because I wouldn't kiss you doesn't give you the right to treat me with disrespect."

She stormed by him, bumping his elbow as she angrily passed. The toes of her sandal caught a loose board, causing her to trip and fall against the pole. She caught herself against it and held tight.

Dizziness suddenly swept over her, and a nauseous sensation crept up from her stomach. If only the rolling would stop. She held her mouth with her hand and slid down the pole. Groaning, she closed her eyes and suddenly wished she'd stayed behind.

Derrick picked her up in his arms. The roaring sound of the ocean dimmed as he carried her inside a room and lay her down on a soft bed.

"If you feel too ill, there is a window behind you, just above your head. It easily slides open. I'll be outside if you need me."

She rolled to her side and moaned, watching him leave. The room moved, literally with the roll of the ship. The dresser along the wall slid, causing a horrible screeching sound every time it moved back and forth. And a small round table with an old wooden chair slid with it in unison, creating a terrible high-pitched screech.

She placed the palm of her hand to her forehead, trying desperately to fight the ill sensation creeping up in her throat. With all the screeching, the rolling, the creaking of old wood, her nerves were completely shot. She wasn't going to be able to hold it back any longer.

With a quick roll, she rose to her knees, grabbed the window with both hands and forced it open. A sudden gush of ocean spray hit her face, soaking her hair and stinging her eyes. But she didn't care as she leaned over the edge, hung her head, and heaved.

She held herself there for what seemed like hours, hoping the nausea wouldn't come back. The ocean mist felt good against her, cooling the fires of her ailing sensation.

She probably would have stayed in that position if Derrick hadn't pulled her back inside half asleep, moaning for him to leave her there and let her die. She lay down and closed her eyes, and within moments fell into a sickened sleep.

•

The sunlight through the window woke her. It wasn't a peaceful wake, but at least the ship wasn't rolling anymore, finally taking to a calmer sea.

She rose from the bed, still feeling a bit run down but much better than she felt at the beginning of the trip. She wondered how long she'd been sleeping.

She made her way to the door and began to open it, but when she heard Derrick speaking to someone outside, she stopped. Curious, she held her ear to the door and listened.

"The dear soul is hard to find, but I will do what I can," she heard a woman speak clearly, a gurgling sound prominent in her breathy voice.

"You know the importance of this," Derrick said urgently.

"Indeed, dear Guardian, indeed," she replied. "I will do as you desire once your part is fulfilled."

A strange silence crept over the cabin. Katherine waited for a moment, wanting desperately to hear more, but not another word was spoken. At first she thought the woman had left, but when she suddenly heard footsteps treading quickly toward her, she began to panic.

With a leap in her step, she made her way back to the bed. She'd only had time to sit down and cover her legs when the door to the cabin swung open wide.

Derrick stood in the doorway, a frown lingering on his face. He stared at her for a moment, and then motioned for her to come outside.

The cool breeze billowed through the cabin, causing her to shiver. She pulled the blanket off the bed and draped it around her shoulders as she stepped outside.

He stood at the port side, arms folded over his chest as he waited on her. He looked miffed, possibly a little confused, or maybe both as she came to stand before him.

He eyed her peculiarly. "Ezra would like to meet you," he said, the manner of his voice worried and somewhat baffled.

"Ezra?" Katherine asked curiously, glancing around the ship for the woman she'd heard speak just a few moments before.

Derrick gave out a sigh and stepped to the side. He turned around and nodded his head toward the edge of the ship. "She's there."

Katherine walked closer, fearing the possibility of what she'd see. There had already been so many unbelievable things, though she assumed it to all be a dream. But since she'd found herself in Derrick's arms the night before, she began to believe. She wanted to.

She walked to the edge of the ship and peered down, and suddenly lost her breath. She quickly turned away from the vision of this fictitious being lying beautifully on a platform rock, blissfully smiling at her.

"What is it?" Derrick asked, grasping her wrists in his hands. "What have you done to her?" he yelled angrily over the edge.

"She's a mermaid," Katherine whispered, wiping shocked tears with the back of her hand. "No, I'm okay with this."

"Are you sure?" he asked anxiously.

Katherine nodded and turned to face her fears.

Ezra smiled, her eyes a bright blue sky underneath long white locks of hair. She lay on her side, caressing the rock lovingly, naked and surprisingly very much like a woman. The only hint she was a mermaid was the deep blue shade of her finned hands and feet, and a strange mask of gills along her jaw-line.

She was beautiful. Katherine caught herself staring at her, wishing she looked like her, wanting desperately to be her. But when Derrick came to stand at her side, placing his hand on her shoulder, it broke the envious enchantment.

"What do you want with me?"

"Ah," Ezra said, sitting up on the rock. She pulled her knees to her chest and giggled. "You are just as I imagined, beautiful, strong, and proud."

"What are you talking about?"

"I heard the rumors you were here, but I never dreamed I would ever get to finally meet you. But here you are, the vision of your mother so true in your features."

Katherine glanced up at Derrick. "What is she talking about?"

"I'm not certain," he said with a shrug. "Mermaids are known to lie on occasion. So quite possibly she's playing a game."

"Have I ever played games with you before?" Ezra asked him. "Have I ever lied to you?"

Derrick shook his head but again shrugged. "We haven't seen each other in a long while, Ezra. Things change and yet I'm sure you've taken on the aspects of your sisters. They are nothing but fibbing fish."

Ezra stood up and stomped her blue-finned foot. Though terribly angry, Katherine could tell she was quite hurt by the look in her eye before she swiftly dove into the sea.

Derrick walked to the aft and began to hoist the anchor. He'd hurt the poor girl's feelings. And if he'd been so rude with her, she would not have hesitated to slap him.

"I can't believe you said such a terrible thing to her," she said as she joined him at the helm.

"She already gave me what I wanted," he replied, turning the wheel slightly to the right. "If she wasn't lying about it, then Mila should be due north about an hour from here."

"What did she mean?" she asked him as she held on to the side of the benched seat. "She said I looked just like my mother. She was about to tell me until you rudely sent her away."

"She was lying to you," he replied coolly as he straightened the ship out.

He latched the wheel, locking it securely into place. With a quick step, he made his way across the deck, leaving her standing there, speculating alone.

She knew he was hiding something from her, and something terribly important by the way he glanced at her before disappearing through the cabin door. Something had definitely changed in his attitude, dramatically, and she was sure it had something to do with his conversation with Ezra.

She shivered as an eerie sensation crept over her. And inspecting the small window beside the cabin door, she found him watching her, eyes glowing slightly. It was awkward, the way he stared. He seemed cold, unlike the man that wanted to kiss her just that morning. If only she'd awoken a few moments earlier, she could've heard more of their conversation.

As she pulled her eyes away from his, a large shadow crossed the ship. It briefly blocked the sun from her skin, causing a shudder. She quickly glanced up in the sky, trying to spot whatever it was flying over her, but there was nothing, not even a cloud.

With quickness in her step, she walked toward the cabin. Her skin crawled with dread when she saw Derrick walk out the door and join her underneath the main mast just as the wind abruptly stopped. The sails were silenced, and the only sound came from the calm waves of the sea, gently rippling around the ship.

She found her way to his side and grabbed hold of his arm. "What's going on?" she whispered, eyeing the quiet sails.

"You should go inside," he said.

It may have sounded like a request, but she knew it was a demand. Whatever was out here with them certainly had him spooked as well, but she wasn't about to miss anything else.

"I'm staying here with you."

He sighed, but gripped her hand tight in his as they walked farther out onto the deck. She followed in his steps, never missing one until he suddenly stopped.

"Get behind me," he barked his order as he pulled her until she was behind him.

"What is it?" she asked when he let go of her hand.

He walked toward the steps leading to the bow of the ship, just above the cabin. He motioned with his hand for her to stay put, and with the serious look on his face, she did as he asked.

As he neared the steps, her eyes wandered aimlessly, looking for whatever had interrupted their journey. Her eyes landed on Derrick's back, but a slight movement above him caught her eye, forcing her to look up.

On the lower branch of the first mast sat a large dark figure, perched like a bird. It stood up as Derrick walked by making it look very ominous and quite horrifying as it peered down at him.

"Derrick!" she yelled loudly as she ran toward him, pointing at the figure. "There!"

The figure extended wings as big as the sail, and quickly leapt off the mast. It flew around the ship, hissing as if it were a snake, and screeching as if it was an eagle ready to dive onto its prey. And by the look it gave Derrick, he was the one it was after.

He backed down the steps as it landed on the bow of the ship with a loud thud. The wood underneath its large feathered feet cracked and bent as it stood there, staring at him in discontent. It stepped up off the splinters and ruffled its feathers like a bird getting ready to sit in its nest, and then it did just that—frumpily sat down.

It pushed its enormous wings back and revealed long legs covered in black feathers to its hips. She had the curvy physique of a female, with splendorous dark hair glistening in sunlight as she stared at them with black bird-like eyes. The being was frightening, and not only in a sense she meant them harm, but by the way she looked at Derrick as if he were a meal ready to be served.

He stood in front of Katherine, protecting her, though she knew it wasn't her he needed to worry about. The thing obviously wanted him, and by the way he looked at it, she was beginning to think he felt the same way.

Derrick's eyes began to glow, but it wasn't the color he normally carried. Darkness shrouded them, and a black mist danced a path to the being on the bow of the ship.

Katherine took him by the hand and pulled when he began walking toward it, but he wouldn't stop. "Derrick!" she yelled, but he wouldn't listen as he continued up the wooden stairs.

She stepped in front of him, but he shoved her aside as if she were nothing more than an obstacle. The being called him somehow—an enchantment through a song she obviously couldn't hear. And it suddenly dawned on her what this terrible thing was. It was Mila, the Siren they'd been searching for, and Derrick was falling right into her charm.

Katherine turned to her with pleading eyes. "Please," she said. "He came here to ask for your help."

Nothing happened, no response, not even a look came from her as she welcomed Derrick into her arms. He suddenly fell limp as she opened her mouth, revealing two sets of very large, and quite sharp, canine teeth. Katherine realized she meant to eat him right there, in front of her.

"Please," she pleaded again, falling to her knees in front of her. "There has to be something I can do. I'll do anything you ask of me if you'll just spare him!"

Mila stopped and looked down at her. A chill crept over her body and she began to tremble, thinking she'd now averted the hunger on her.

"You would do anything for this man?" she asked, and Katherine cringed slightly at her unusual high-pitched chirp.

"I'll do anything," she replied, trying her best to meet her beady eyes.

"Foolish woman," she said, dropping Derrick carelessly to the floor.

He rolled toward the steps, but Katherine quickly grabbed hold of his shirt before he fell over and onto the deck. His eyes were closed but a grin lingered on his ignorant face.

"Derrick," she said, urgently shaking him, trying to wake him from his sleep, but he remained lifeless.

She found the courage to look up into Mila's eyes yet again. With an outraged stare, she stood up on her feet and boldly faced her.

"What did you do to him?"

"You may have his carcass, but his soul will remain with me," she cackled, twittering her voice like a bird.

"No!" Katherine yelled at her, feeling tears work into her eyes. "He doesn't belong to you."

She fell to her knees and clutched his shirt in her hands. She shook him gently, and then hard, trying to get him to wake up, but he wouldn't. He only lay there while this horrible thing was about to fly off with his essence, and furthermore, leaving her out in the middle of the sea alone.

She frantically looked around, and eyed the axe conveniently hanging on the banister, just above Derrick's body. If she could find the courage and strength to swing it, she'd chop off her head before she could leave the ship.

Katherine drew in a deep breath just as Mila turned her back preparing to take flight. She quickly leapt to her feet and lunged for the axe. With panic in her breath, she pulled the weapon off the banister, and turned around ready to face her fear.

As Mila spread her dark wings, she lifted the axe over her head. It was heavy and more so than she thought, but she swung it with all her might. She cringed, closing her eyes as the axe made contact with something, but she was afraid to look.

Mila let out an agonizingly loud screech, making Katherine drop the axe from her hands and fall to her knees. She covered her ears and conveniently placed her eyes on the item on the floor in front of her. A gold chain necklace held a round red gem slightly cracked down the center. It was beautiful, mesmerizing as it glistened in the sunlight.

"Where did it go?" Mila screeched, frantically searching her neck. "My pendant is gone!"

Katherine quickly grabbed the necklace and stood up. She backed toward the edge of the ship, holding it out in her hand with a smirk, knowing she finally had leverage on this horrible creature.

"Give it back!" Mila demanded as she stomped toward her, rather horrified.

Terrified herself, Katherine positioned the necklace over the water and gave a short nervous laugh through her nose. "You won't get it back! Not until you return what you've taken from me."

Mila suddenly stopped, just short of an arm's length. She reached for the necklace, but Katherine retracted her arm farther over the water.

"Make another advance and I'll drop it," she warned, finding intrigue in her own threatening voice.

Mila drew in a deep breath, her mouth opening to a morbidly large hole as she inhaled. Her sharp teeth seemed to extend outward as she breathed in, causing Katherine to take an uncertain step back, but she wasn't about to give in.

She watched as she held her breath, making her pale face turn a shade of red. But just as Katherine thought she'd pass out from lack of breath, she quickly let it out.

The sound was excruciating. A scream like no other came from her mouth, hitting Katherine at full force. She shut her eyes tight as her hair whipped back and her skin tightened, but it wasn't going to make her waver a bit. She held fast and rigid until the scream finally ended.

Opening her eyes, she caught Mila reaching again for the necklace. But this time she leaned over the edge.

"Don't drop my pendant," she suddenly cried, weeping loudly and dramatically in the palm of her hands.

"Then offer me a trade," Katherine said, thankful to hear she was finally backing down, and hopefully was going to cooperate.

"My gem is worth a thousand of these pitiful creatures," she said as she walked back up to the bow of the ship.

"And he's worth more to me," Katherine retorted, as she made her way to Derrick's side. She bent down to him, holding her gaze stern to make sure Mila stayed back.

"Then a deal I shall make," she said in solemn defeat.

Though her voice was sincere, her face was telling a different story. Something vindictive played in her eyes—a plan, concocted by conniving delight gave Katherine a horrible chill.

•

"The diamond you seek is very rare
and can only be found in one devious lair.
Swim past his throne to the jeweled hall,
past the stables into darkness you fall.
Precious gems light your path
to Poseidon's chamber of unsettling wrath.
The black gem lies beneath his bed.
Retrieve it for me or his son stays dead."

•

Katherine observed her, unable to comprehend why she'd become so poetic all of the sudden. But she'd do whatever was necessary to save Derrick's soul.

"If I do this, you'll release him?" she asked, eyeing her peculiarly.

"I will release him as promised," she replied, surprisingly in an earnest tone.

"You have to promise you'll answer all his questions too," she added carefully.

"No," she snapped. "I won't agree to this demand."

"Then no deal," Katherine stepped back to the edge of the ship and held the necklace over the water, this time serious about dropping it.

"Fine!" Mila yelled, and then let out a long sigh. "I'll answer all questions asked. Then you both will leave me alone for eternity." She turned slightly, casting a grim smile across her face. "That is, if you survive the retrieval. The god of the sea is rather temperamental and preys on young beautiful maidens such as yourself."

"I'll be fine," she said angrily, draping the necklace around her neck. "So how do I get there from here?"

Mila quickly turned around. With a flip of her wrist, she sent Katherine over the edge of the ship.

She plunged down into the water, unable to catch her weight to drift back to the surface. She fell deeper and faster through darkening water, terrifyingly dragged down by the red pendant. Panic spread through her as she struggled not to breathe, but it was coming on fast.

Watching as the bottom of the ship disappeared and there was nothing to fix her eyes on, she felt her tears pouring out into the sea. And then panic turned to terror when she felt somebody grasp her arm and pull on her, but it was too late to struggle as she drew in a deep gurgling breath, and let the water into her lungs.

With a light skip in her step, she made her way around their landing zone, gently swiping her hand through the blades of grass. And with a short glance back, she motioned Katherine to follow her further into the meadow.

Katherine quickly stood up. With a glance back at the sea, she wondered if following her was the right thing to do. She really needed to find the gem before it was too late, but something was telling her to go on and find out what this terrible secret was.

Darkened by the woods, Ezra stopped and turned to face her. Her smile still lingered as she leaned in close and breathed deeply. And as if she were catching the scent from a beautiful flower, she hummed.

It was a very odd thing to do. But everything about this journey was beyond the norm, and a bout of impatience hit her.

Ezra leaned back, standing straight with her arms behind her back. She clasped her fingers together and tightened to a straight-lipped poise.

"You must first promise you won't tell anyone I told you."

"I promise," she said directly.

Ezra took her by the arm and continued to pull her down the dark path. The trees thickened around them as they walked, giving Katherine a chill as it blocked out the remnants of sunlight, but it left her mind as Ezra began to speak.

"Gods are forbidden to covet their kind for too much destruction tainted their offspring. But she fell in love with a god, and they secretly conceived a child. Fearing the child's heart would be dark, she consumed it and then hid it away inside a black diamond. It was an ultimate sacrifice, for it took all of her will to fulfill such a task. It would take years to replenish the magic she lost, so she left our world to graze in heaven's fields. And for many years she lived as the horned beast, guarded only by what was believed to be a simple Atlantean—a guardian with no name."

Ezra shivered slightly. "She had not planned on the Outsiders' magic becoming as powerful as to pluck her from the golden fields. They stole her away into the human world, and though her guardian followed, he was not powerful enough to pull her back through the rift. The only thing he could do was sever her horn and assume his immortal place."

"They tortured him," Katherine said solemnly. "They locked him away in a box and dumped him into the sea as his punishment."

Mila's necklace began to glow causing Ezra's eyes to widen. She quickly jerked it off Katherine's neck and tossed it as far as she could into the trees behind them.

"Why did you do that?" Katherine asked in a panic as she watched it fall onto a high branch. "I need to take it back to Mila in trade for Derrick's soul!"

Ezra took her by the arm and began walking down the path, a little faster and a lot more leery of their surroundings. "I did not realize you were wearing her necklace. She must know where we are now."

Katherine quit struggling and quickly followed Ezra. Glancing back at the pendant, still emitting light as it hung from the branch, she began to panic.

"Give me the quick version, Ezra," she said as she saw a large dark figure land underneath the tree. "Since I've always had the diamond, does that mean I'm her child?"

The light of the pendant turned to shadow with the cover of a hand, and she knew exactly who it was. Mila had indeed found them.

"Things are not what they seem, Katherine," Ezra said, breathing fast as they ran away from Mila's stomping chase. "They will kill you for no reason!"

Katherine ran straight into a solid body, stopping her immediately. She screamed, struggling hard to break loose, but the hands holding her turned her abruptly and cupped her mouth.

"Katherine," he spoke loudly in her ear. "Please stop fighting me!"

Her breath was frantic, but when she heard Derrick's voice, she stopped her fight and turned to see him. He let his hand loose from her mouth and flashed a dashing grin.

"You're alive?" she asked as if seeing him for the first time in years. Tears came to her eyes, but it wasn't from relief, it was from the confusion from everything happening and everything she'd just heard.

Ezra's voice echoed in her mind, and she backed away from him, shaking her head in disbelief and meaning to quickly get away. And though he didn't make any sudden advances to catch her, he followed her just beyond a grasp.

"Don't be afraid of me, Katherine. All I need is the diamond," he said.

"I didn't get it," she replied with a brief glance at Ezra who had fallen to the ground, obviously fearing what was going to happen.

"What did she tell you?" he asked worriedly. "I told you before she is not to be trusted."

"She didn't tell me anything," she lied, stepping back until a large body of soft dark feathers caught her. A gasp escaped her trembling lips, realizing she'd just backed into Mila.

Derrick stopped in front of her and gazed into her eyes. He brought his palm to her cheek and touched her lightly.

"You lied to me," she whispered, closing her eyes as more tears worked into them. "You stole my gem because you mean to kill me. Isn't this what you've planned all along?"

"I would never do anything to hurt you," he replied with a sigh, and dropped his hand to his side. He stood for a moment, gathering in the way she held her terrified eyes.

"White hair doesn't suit you," he said in an irritated voice, placing his eyes on Ezra. "Turn her back before she's stuck like this forever."

"But she has until morning," Ezra argued in mischief. "It will be less painful."

"Do it now!" His demanding voice made Katherine jump.

"Just go back to your decrepit old ship and leave me alone!"

"My ship is not decrepit and old, it is merely overused," he said as he strode to Ezra's side and picked her up off the ground with a jerk of her arm. She let out a painful shout as he dragged her across the ground until he impatiently shoved her to face Katherine.

"She is beginning to think like a mermaid. Remove the spell," he ordered angrily.

And defy her true calling?"

Derrick nudged her forward again and Katherine could see the solemn defeat in her eyes.

"I am sorry," Ezra whispered low enough only she could hear. "I only wanted to protect you."

Katherine's fingers and toes suddenly began to tingle as if they'd fallen asleep. The sensation was so strong, she slumped to her knees cringing as it grew into a painful throb. She curled up on the dirt path, shutting her eyes and trying to endure the pain without bursting into tears.

The onlookers studied her with unscrupulous eyes. And not knowing which ones were true, she began to resent them all.

The itch on her jaw-line dissipated, leaving her face smooth and pale. Her dark hair returned, blending into the shadows of the trees. And with the conclusion of fingers and toes, the pain finally went away.

She found it easier to breathe without gills. As if she'd suddenly surfaced from the depths of the water, she drew in a deep breath.

"Much better," Derrick said as he held his hand out for her to take.

Somehow, her mind seemed to clear, and curiously the trust for him returned as she accepted his hand. She held her arm across her breasts, trembling as the chill of the oncoming night hit her skin. Tired, hungry, and still quite confused, she let out an aching moan.

Derrick quickly pulled off his shirt and gently clothed her with it. He drew her close to his chest, warming her body with his. And as he led her down the pathway, leaving Ezra remorsefully on the ground, a profound thought struck her. She desperately wanted to leave this place and somehow find her way home.

Chapter Ten

Three days had come and gone faster than the blink of an eye, but Katherine felt like she was stuck in quicksand. *Knee deep and sinking*, she thought miserably as she sat in the small house staring out the window at the rising sun.

Derrick had left two days ago without a word where he was going, though she had suspicions he was going after the diamond. They hadn't spoken to each other much since he'd found her in the woods with Ezra, but she wished he'd at least told her when he'd be back.

Mortin had brought meals to her every day at the same time. He was very kind, keeping her company for a little while as she ate, and offering her a genuine grin when she looked at him. But every time she asked him about Derrick, he'd pick up and leave her alone. And though he remained quiet, she could see the apprehension in his eyes.

She began to feel like a prisoner though Derrick never mandated her to stay inside the house. She was free to wander around the city as long as the orb he'd given her followed her wherever she went, stressing it was only for her protection.

She glanced at the shining black orb quietly humming like a tiny mechanical engine as it hovered over her right shoulder. It always seemed to observe her, lighting her way in the night and watching over her when she slept.

It was there every morning, waiting for her to get out of bed. And the only time it left her side was when she bathed.

Strange little thing, she thought. It seemed alive, suspended in the air. Sometimes she'd catch it beautifully twinkling, or turning away whenever she looked at it. It was a crazy notion, but sometimes she imagined it had a mind of its own, although she'd never spoken a word to it to find out.

"Does the sun always shine here?" she asked the orb, feeling a little silly for doing so. "I've never seen it rain."

She watched it carefully, but nothing changed.

"I wonder where Mortin is," she said, finding talking to it helped soothe her mood anyway. "What I would give for a bowl of fruit, maybe even hotcakes from the breakfast joint down the street from my apartment. Boy do I miss being home." She glanced at it again, giving it a short grin. "The things I've taken for granted. But you wouldn't understand it now would you, my little friend?"

The hum of the orb suddenly changed. As if it became excited, it began to spin, making short twittering noises as it turned.

It circled her once, and in a flash, flew out the window. It hurried through the courtyard, dodging plants and ducking through the fountain until it finally left the gate.

"Well isn't this interesting," she whispered in fascination, wondering what in the world had just happened.

In a few moments time, she saw the orb slowly float through the gate, a white bowl made of clay wobbling on its little round body. It carefully made its way through the window and set itself down on the sill in front of her.

Katherine grinned as she lifted the bowl. "Thank you," she said graciously when she found three beautifully ripened strawberries inside.

The orb twittered and hummed as it took its place over her right shoulder. Though it seemed to go back to its normal hover, the light burned much brighter than before.

"Now I know you understand me. I wonder if you can talk back," she said eyeing it inquisitively and hoping it'd say something, but it only hummed. "So you can't talk to me then," she said, shaking her head no as its light dimmed. "Well," she continued as she took a bite of her strawberry. "I'll talk and you can listen. How does that sound?"

The light blinked, offering her its answer with a louder hum.

"As much as I love talking to you, I wish you could tell me where Derrick is."

An eerie sound suddenly came from the center of the room, and the tub began to bubble, emitting the same scent it did every morning. She'd gotten used to it now, finding it rather odd, but never stepping foot near it until it was finished doing its morning ritual.

This time though, she seriously felt the need to bathe. And setting the strawberries back down on the window sill, she followed the scent to the tub.

Slightly dazed, she disrobed and stepped inside the water. It was unbelievably warm and the bubbles massaged her body, coaxing her into imminent relaxation. She leaned her head back against the wall and let her eyelids fall, but it was only brief.

A faint humming interrupted her meditation. Opening her eyes, she glanced around the room. The orb was missing. She could hear it, but she couldn't see it anywhere.

"Where are you?" she asked, hoping it would show itself, but it didn't.

A sense of dread swept over her as she rose from the tub and stepped out. She shivered at the thought that someone held it back, watching as she slipped on her robe.

"Who's there?" she asked as she tied the straps around her waist. "I know you're here. So you might as well show yourself."

A shadow crept along the back wall. It didn't hold much shape as its footsteps moved soundlessly across the stone floor.

Katherine moved toward the bed, watching as it headed for the front door. And though she was terribly concerned by its presence, she found the courage to speak.

"Wait," she called out in a trembling voice. "What are you doing here?"

It did as she asked and stopped near the door. She hadn't planned on it turning and coming back, but it did, quietly and eerily.

As it moved, she heard the humming of the orb coming from the armoire beside her. She hurriedly opened the doors and let the little light, now blazing an angry red, out of its wood prison.

She watched as it found the dark stranger and began circling it, humming and flying around it like an annoying little bee. It struck her as funny, though she should be running from this ominous being instead of being amused.

The shadow huddled down in the floor, swatting at the little annoyance that kept up its attack. She chuckled as the comedy scene played before her eyes, but she knew she had to find out what this thing was and what it wanted.

"Orb," she called out, catching its attention. "It's okay. I don't think it means us harm."

The orb immediately stopped and returned to her. She looked at the shadow sitting in the floor, gaining composure as it awaited her to speak.

"What are you?" she asked, carefully making her way close to the front door in case she needed to quickly escape.

"I am a messenger," it whispered.

"A messenger?" she asked curiously. "Who sent you?"

"The Ferryman."

She glanced briefly at the orb and then returned her attention to the shadow, arching her brow in instant curiosity. "You mean the Ferryman from the river Styx?"

"Yes," it whispered with an obvious sigh of relief that it didn't have to explain itself further. "He wanted you to have this."

She watched as the shadow suddenly took on a shape. Two feet protruded from its dark matter and walked toward her. It extended its liquid-like form until it brought forth a human hand. It held something in its grasp and waited for her to raise her hand and accept it.

She bravely raised her arm and showed her palm. The item dropped and immediately latched onto her skin. Her eyes immediately widened just as her lips stretched into a smile. "You found my diamond."

"The jewel of life and death," it whispered cordially. "From his lips, to mine ears. This warning he passes to you—leave Atlantis now, but do not let the gem leave your grasp. My work here is done. My soul is free."

The shadow suddenly rose into the air and disappeared, leaving her standing in complete awe. She gazed at the black jewel in her hand, not knowing what to think, and furthermore, what to do with this unholy message.

The door to the house suddenly opened wide, startling her in a terrible way. With her heart in her throat, she sat down on the bed trying to catch her breath as she glared at her intruder.

A rather pale and quite scruffy looking Derrick walked in. He stared at her with tired eyes. And his unshaven face covered the disappointment lingering in his frown.

The orb doused its angry energy, quickly returning its normal shade of silver. Katherine thought it was possibly hiding the fact it had showed itself to her, for Derrick's sake.

"Where have you been?" she asked him as he made his way to the bed. "You look like you haven't slept in days," she continued, ignoring his silence.

He fell onto the bed, halfway covering his body as he laid his head on the pillow and immediately shut his eyes. Within moments he fell asleep, leaving her sitting beside him, eyes running over his fatigued appearance.

She desperately needed to find out where he'd been, and if her suspicions were true. Quite possibly the answer was on his ship, but she despised going back to that dreadful thing.

She quietly dressed and made her way outside the house, careful not to disturb him. Happy to see the orb was following her, she hurried down the street.

"I have to know," she whispered to the orb. "I imagine he's been trying to find my gem, but I'm trying not to believe it's for the same purpose Ezra told me about."

The orb twittered lightly, agreeing with her as they made their way across the pier. The ragged ship sat just as before at the end, but this time it looked worse, much worse.

The front mast was broken in half, and all the sails were loosely hanging from them. Ripped and frayed at the edges, it was as if some giant cat had used it as a scratching post, or it had been through one ruthless hurricane. And strangely, a dark cloud hovered over it releasing a steady mist as everything surrounding it basked in sunlight.

"This doesn't look good," she said as she carefully made her way up the ramp and hopped down onto the wet deck. The wood cracked beneath her feet, and she swore the thing would start to sink by the way it creaked.

Swallowing down her nervous twitch, she stepped forward and headed toward the cabin. She trembled as the cold mist bizarrely turned to a steady rain, making her hurry to the door and step inside, drenched and shivering. Cursing mildly, she pulled her hair to the side and wrung it out.

The room was empty as she wandered around the cabin searching for a clue. Besides an old map lying on the small dresser along the wall, the only other thing catching her eye was the colorful rainbow outside the window.

She looked at the map and caught sight of a familiar design. The pyramid, marked with two eyes circled in pencil was placed in the center of the city, just where it stood now.

She picked it up to take with her and study further, but as she held it in her hands, she noticed markings on the back. Flipping it over, she found another map, but this one covered a vast sea leading to an image of a throne with the words "Poseidon's Chamber" written below it.

It was true then. He'd definitely gone after the gem, and by the looks of him and this ruined ship, they'd fought for it.

She rolled the map, tucked it under her arm, and then turned to leave, but abruptly stopped. She found Derrick blocking the doorway frowning in discontent. Completely startled that she hadn't heard him come in, she cleared her throat nervously.

"What are you doing here?" he asked.

"I—" she stammered, glancing past him as if trying to find an excuse. She felt the map slide from her arm.

"This doesn't belong to you," he said as he unrolled it and set it back down on the table.

"I was only trying to find out where you'd been," she said stubbornly.

He didn't reply, but looked as if he were contemplating. The tiredness showed in his bloodshot eyes.

"You told me before, you would never lie to me," she continued, hoping to weigh on his emotion to get him to talk. "Should I be worried for my life?"

By the way he looked at her, solemn and obviously frustrated she could tell he understood why she asked the question. And it became apparent to her that Ezra had told her the truth. He had indeed meant to kill her.

She watched as he walked to the table stroking his shadowed jaw, leaving the door clear, and without hesitation she dashed outside into the downpour. Clutching the black jewel tightly in her hand, she quickly ran to the starboard side of the ship and climbed up on the ramp. Drenched from the rain, she made her way down to the pier, and found comfort when the orb joined her again.

The warmth of the sun felt good as she leaned over her knees, trying to catch her panicking breath. The orb hummed in her ear, dancing up and down as if telling her not to stop, but she had to. Out of breath and full of tears, she stood at the bottom of the ramp and watched Derrick walk down to her side.

"I'm not going to run from you anymore," she cried.

Derrick placed his hand on her shoulder, and heaved a surrendering sigh. "I went to speak with my father," he admitted as he found a seat near the ramp of the ship and slumped down onto it. "I begged him to give it to me, but he refused."

Katherine wiped tears from her face, listening intently. "And what would you do if he had given it to you?"

It was the first time she'd seen him grin since he'd come back, and her heart melted, finding her attraction for him return as he gazed at her with somber eyes. And although he was as handsome as ever in his gruff appearance, she couldn't let her guard down just yet.

"Ezra told you what it's for, did she?" he asked with a smirk. "It's okay if she did, for you have the right to know. I should not have tried to silence her, but I wanted to find a way to tell you myself."

She sat down beside him. "Ezra told me you mean to use the jewel to retrieve something inside me."

His face went pale. Her knowledge of the situation obviously upset him, but she knew he had to face this, just as she needed to courageously face whatever the outcome.

"She didn't have enough time to tell me everything about it so please," she pleaded with him, "tell me everything you know."

He immediately fell to his knees and took her hands in his. Kneeling before her, he shook his head in awful shame. "I can find a way to hide you from this." He grew excited as he stood up and lifted her to her feet. "Stay with me, Katherine," he pleaded. "I will take you where no eyes will see and no ears will hear—a place where you and the gem will be safe."

"I don't know Derrick," she said. "Who's to say someone else won't make an attempt on my life?"

"I give my word nobody will ever harm you. Besides," he said with hesitation, "I'm the only one who knows the words, so it would be my duty alone to perform your sacrifice."

Katherine shivered at his words. To think she was nothing more than a sacrifice was terribly unnerving.

"Don't worry," he said in a reassuring voice. "Stay with me and everything will be fine."

"Stay with you?" she asked seeing the sincerity in his gaze. "Why should I?"

With a quick yank of her hand he pulled her against him. It was rather frightening, the way he stared into her eyes, deeply penetrating her in a way she couldn't resist the sudden flutter inside her. Holding her still and palming her cheek, he caressed her gently. He touched his forehead to hers, and her heart immediately sank.

Though she enjoyed the way he touched her, she moved away. His embrace lingered for a moment as she walked to the end of the pier and ambled up the street toward the house, glancing behind her from time to time to see if he was there. He followed, never removing his eyes from her and never advancing into chase.

"I'll agree to stay for a little while," she said coolly as he followed her through the front door of the house. "But I can't promise I'll stay long. I'm not sure I can leave everything I know behind."

"You mean like Ty," he replied intently.

"Oh," she said, suddenly remembering him. "I can't imagine what he's going through right now."

With a confused glance, Derrick nodded and took off his wet shirt. He tossed it into the floor, a proud smirk playing on his lips. "You are not my prisoner," he said as he took off his pants. "If you choose to go home, I'll allow it. All I ask of you is to give this more thought before you decide."

She quickly turned away wishing she hadn't seen his strong, masculine body and the way he'd stepped up into the tub, flexing beautifully. Yes, he could definitely make her forget for a little while. But as hard as it was to decline such a man, she knew it was for the best. For if he actually did turn on her, it'd be easier for her to deal with resentment, rather than fight a broken heart.

Chapter Eleven

They walked through the halls of the university. It was a magnificent sight to see, and one Katherine would never forget no matter where her travels ended.

The architecture was defined, something she could see with Plato in mind. Arched sandstone ceilings held by large solid pillars, etched beautifully by masterful architects. Natural marble floors shined magnificently underneath her feet as she walked through open walkways soaking sunlight into the main halls.

She gathered Socrates stood in the same rooms she'd walked through, writing his stories of the Atlanteans so many deemed untrue. People would never believe her in modern times either, most likely locking her away in an asylum if she spoke of this with as much sincerity as he had.

Though she hoped to go home soon, she did find she was enjoying her stay now. And she definitely enjoyed Derrick's attention, the way he stared at her, smiling considerately, desperately trying to make up for the distress he'd caused her.

Whispers and echoes reverberated around her as scholars taught children as young as three and as old as grandparents, the academics of math, science, and even world history. And all had makings to be magic users, laborers, and even architects. As acolytes of prophets, mystics, and unworldly geniuses, they believed in each other without selfishness, making the learning experience much more effective than a standard school.

Derrick told her he'd studied the art of nature as well as war. He'd been chosen to be Koran's guardian at his graduation, finding it a true honor to be picked out of twenty other very gifted students.

"The chosen needed to be strong, not only in mind, but in body as well," he'd told her on the way down the university steps to the beach.

Katherine held her sandals in her hands as they walked. She'd listened to everything, finding intrigue over the slightest unimaginable thing, including an actual Kraken living near the rocks beyond the school. He also told her of a Cyclops, who apparently preyed on evil men, and fell in love with each woman that crossed his path.

"A scholar with an eye for women made his bed with a goddess of war," he said. "When she caught him looking at another woman, she stole his eye and banished him to the Island Plains."

"Where is that?"

Derrick grinned as they stepped onto the sandy beach. "We will go there now, for it is where we'll stay from now on." He took her by the hand and pulled her with him. "I hope you don't mind riding a horse."

"I've never ridden one before."

He stopped just at the brink of a pathway leading up the side of the mountain. A puzzled expression worked over him as he looked at her.

"You've never ridden a horse before?"

"No," she replied. "But I've ridden in a carriage pulled by one."

He stood for a moment in thought. "It's not a big deal," he said as he returned his walk up the path. "You can ride with me."

"Well," she said as she began to lose her breath from the steep incline of the hill. "I think I'll be fine, but whatever you think. My feet are aching, and I wish I'd brought hiking boots with me. How much farther do we need to walk?"

He laughed again, stopping his trudge up hill. "You're beginning to sound like a troll."

She stopped just before him, lowering her brows into a glare. "A troll?"

"Yes," he said with a chuckle. "They're nasty giants that complain about everything, though I don't much blame them. They work in the fields all year long, harvesting food for our markets. Not very smart, and rather smelly, but they're very efficient. We may meet one on the way."

"You use them like slaves then?" she asked angrily, feeling a bit goaded for being compared to one.

"We reward them very well."

He placed his hands on her shoulders and gently squeezed. His eyes sparkled in the sunlight, and she suddenly caught herself in them. She shivered as he lifted his hand to her temple and swiped a stray hair from her eye.

"But you are no troll," he said as he brushed his fingers across her cheek and let go. He took her by the hand, turned around, and began climbing again.

The short break had given her a chance to catch her breath, but he'd made her lose it again with his sensitive touch. Her heart pounded and her palms began to sweat as she let go of his hand and picked up the pace making it to the top of the mountain before him.

But when she turned and found his eyes caressing her, she was thankful she'd worn a lovely white sleeveless chiton, for the day was getting hot, and the way he looked was making it worse.

His muscular chest showed beautifully underneath his thin white long-sleeved shirt, buttoned only half way. His legs were strong in a pair of dark pants tucked perfectly into his high boots. And his long flowing black hair brought out his turquoise eyes, making her attraction for him soar into a tremendous moan of delight.

The bandit in him stole her heart again making her, just for a moment, forget he'd wanted to kill her just a week ago.

"Put a sock in it," she whispered as he came to stand beside her, grinning somewhat mischievously.

"Is something wrong?" he asked.

"No," she said immediately turning away, completely embarrassed by her sensations of lust.

"This way," he said motioning her to follow.

He led her into an area thick with brush and tall weeds. The earth was hard and dry, and vines grew sporadic over the ground causing simple hazards for walking in sandals. She carefully stepped over them, losing her pace as Derrick began to pull ahead.

"Wait for me," she shouted, catching his attention before he got too far. "I'm not wearing boots you know."

He chuckled as he made his way back to her. With an amused grunt, he picked her up in his arms.

"I didn't mean for you to carry me," she groaned.

He began walking toward a wooded area, pure amusement

lingering on his lips. If she didn't know any better, she'd have thought he'd planned all along to capture her in his arms.

"The horses are up ahead," he said, ignoring her suspicious eyes. "I'll call for one once we're out of danger."

"Danger?" she asked, gripping her arms tighter around his neck.

"Now this is familiar," he said, straining his voice. "I need to stop carrying you through dangerous places for fear you might strangle me to death."

She loosened her grip, noticing the break in the vines as they walked into a small sunlit meadow just before a grove. "You can put me down now."

He did as she asked, but took her by the hand and continued pulling her with him. The seriousness on his face told her not to argue just yet, and she wondered exactly what he was worried about.

"What is this place?" she asked in a hushed voice as they ducked underneath a low tree branch.

"We've entered bear territory," he replied in a low voice. "They usually stay hidden when strangers enter the woods, but they've been known to be temperamental." He grinned at her. "Don't worry. We'll be through very soon."

Katherine heard a low growl come from the woods beside them. The sound sent terrible chills up her spine, making her tighten her grip on his hand.

"The bears are much different here than in your world," he continued as they tromped through high grass. "They're bigger."

Her eyes swelled in fear as she glanced around, huddling closer to him. The thought of being attacked by a large vicious animal, ending her endeavor in the middle of nowhere didn't strike her as an adventure.

Derrick immediately stopped. With a finger to his lips, he shushed her into an eerie silence as he enforced them to crouch in the middle of the meadow.

She clutched her arms huddling into the crevice of his. He enveloped her, holding her close as they heard loud, thunderous footsteps slowly drawing near.

"What is ...?"

He quickly cupped her mouth with his hand. "Don't make a

sound," he whispered, staring into her eyes as the footfalls neared their poor hiding place in the tall grass. She nodded as he removed his hand from her mouth and gave her a reassuring grin.

"Relax," he whispered. "There is nothing here I can't handle."

"Who goes in my meadow?" A deep, raspy, and rather annoyed voice boomed around them.

Katherine wanted to scream, but refrained as she leapt into Derrick's arms. "What was that?"

"It's okay," Derrick whispered, taking her hands in his. "It's only a troll."

He began to stand, but she pulled him back down and kissed him quickly on the lips "Be careful."

Derrick eyed her, grinning profusely over her sudden affection. He grabbed her by the head, leaned in, and then planted another on her lips. With a pleasured sigh, he bravely stood up to face this being shaking the earth when it walked.

"Gunther!" he yelled in a friendly manner.

Katherine suddenly twisted her lips. He knew the troll by name, announcing himself as if he'd known the thing for years, though he'd acted as if he'd been as nervous as a five-year-old on a roller coaster just moments before.

The thunderous footsteps stopped, giving her balance enough to turn and peek overtop of the grass. Her eyes scanned the being standing before Derrick, towering over him by at least five men.

Large gray feet, clubbed slightly, secreted a scent as foul as anything she'd ever smelled before. Its large arms protruded from broad shoulders, deformed slightly as one arm was longer than the other. She sat still, watching its features move from glowering oddly into a sweet, innocent snarling grin.

Its crooked teeth underneath dark gray lips were startling. And the one eye sat lower than the other, squinting brightly as he looked down at Derrick.

"Me thought you bear," Gunther muttered playfully. "Almost kill you with bare hands."

"And that would not have been pleasurable," Derrick replied, motioning with his hand for her to remain where she was. "I was just passing through your meadow to find my horse. Say," he continued. "You wouldn't happen to have seen my horse around would you?"

"What horse look like?"

"Oh," he said, grinning auspiciously. "He is white and runs very, very fast."

Katherine couldn't help but smile. As manly as Derrick was, she found him terribly cute as he spoke to Gunther like a child, causing her to mistakenly let out a short silent laugh.

"I hear noise," Gunther said quickly crouching into a defensive stance. "It behind you in grass!"

The snarling growl coming from him echoed around the meadow, and Katherine suddenly feared he was going to pounce on her, crushing her with his large smelly feet. She stood up, scared stiff, mouth open ready to scream, but Derrick quickly cupped her mouth.

"Wait, Gunther," he cried out, extending his arm to stop him from leaping on her. "It's only a woman."

"Only a woman?" she asked when he let go of her mouth, a little offended by the way he'd said it.

Gunther looked Katherine over with a curious eye. "She too pretty to be woman." He leaned close and eyed her carefully. "She faerie. Gunther not like faeries."

"Oh," Derrick grinned, taking her gently by the arm. "But you'll like this one. She's as sweet as a flower in bloom, and delicate like the petunias you grow in your garden."

"Flowers die," Gunther said, sighing disappointedly. "They not like Gunther anymore."

"I'm sorry to hear this my friend," he said solemnly. "I know how much they meant to you."

"It not my fault," he said as he glared at Katherine again. "Faeries destroy when Koran leave." He stood up straight, bringing forth a warrior image, proud and relentless, but oddly his eyes remained gentle. "Koran leave and chaos begin. Animals run wild tearing up temple and fight each other. I not see anger like this before. It hurt Gunther to see."

Derrick's face fell in concern as he stroked his jaw in thought. "Interesting."

"Magic leave Atlantis very soon if Koran not come back."

Katherine took hold of Derrick's arm, unsure of Gunther's words. He was obviously in turmoil by the terrible things that had happened to him. Somehow she felt like she'd been the cause, and he was right in assuming it was her fault his flowers had died.

She opened her mouth to speak, to tell him how truly sorry she was, but a horrible growl interrupted her. She turned around to find a rather large brown bear barreling toward her, its mouth open wide, calling out a horrifying charge. Its eyes were on her, black and threatening like it meant to tear her apart.

Too stunned to move, she stood eyes wide in terror. She let out a scream as it stood up, stretching out its large claws, meaning to attack. It lunged forward coming within an inch before she closed her eyes and screamed, knowing she was about to experience enormous pain.

Derrick quickly pulled her away as Gunther swung his arm, knocking the bear back. It flew across the meadow and landed with a thunderous thud on the hard ground.

Gunther jumped toward it and with one hand lifted it up by its neck. "You not be bad," he shouted, tears forming in his malformed eyes as he shook it. "What happen to animals? They all go crazy!"

Katherine huddled in Derrick's arms, trying to catch her breath. She watched Gunther suddenly set the bear down gently on the ground and pat its head as if it were his pet dog.

"He sorry," Gunther called out with his crooked grin. He stomped toward them with the bear at his side. "He not know you, but I tell him."

Katherine held on tight to Derrick as they neared. "And just who did you tell him I was?" she asked as she began brushing off dirt from her backside.

"You are dark ..."

"We must be going!" Derrick yelled, abruptly interrupting him. He chuckled as he grabbed Katherine by the arm, and walked her to the edge of the meadow, glancing back with a nervous grin. "It was nice to see you again, Gunther."

"What did he mean?" Katherine asked, glancing back at Gunther curiously. She found him completely puzzled as he looked down at the bear oddly bowing to them as they disappeared into the woods.

"Don't worry," Derrick said as they carefully walked underneath branches. "We're almost to the field."

She looked at him. The solidity of his movement, seemingly unafraid of anything, he was terribly courageous through everything they'd endured. He was obviously well-known as the guardian to a being that no longer existed in this world, but terribly missed.

If Koran's magic was truly buried inside her somewhere, how could she continue without acknowledging it? To deny Derrick his calling, his destiny to be this guardian would be cruel and unjust, but how could she sacrifice herself for the cause? And exactly what would be the cause she'd die for?

A chill crept over her like many fingers stroking her skin. She shivered, deciding to stop and make a stand. And when they left the dark woods and into a vast field of golden hay waving in a lovely warm breeze, she came to a halt.

Derrick noticed she'd stopped and turned to find her standing still, a look of overwhelming dismay stirring in her blue eyes. With a bewildered glance he faced her, palming her cheek.

"Now what's wrong?" he asked. "You look mystified."

"You need to draw the magic from me," she blurted, feeling oddly contented for doing so. "I understand how important it is. Your world is dying without it."

He stood aghast and pulled his hand away from her. With an apprehensive look, he shook his head.

"You amaze me more everyday," he said. "But I've already told you it's not necessary." He turned around, eyeing the large field. "Now where are those horses?"

"Don't ignore me," she yelled, grabbing him by the arm before he could walk away. "I can't let an entire world suffer. And you heard Gunther; the magic here isn't stable anymore."

"We've already been through this, Katherine. I made a terrible mistake on the ship by letting you go, but there's no reason for you to worry about it any longer. You won't be sacrificed for Koran's sins, or anyone else's for this matter. Besides, once the gem is hidden, nobody will look for it again, and everything will be fine."

"You can't hide me forever."

"Just be quiet!" he stressed, forcefully grabbing her by the arms. "We'll not discuss it further. Do you understand?"

"No," she replied. "I don't."

"It's too damn bad," he said shoving her slightly when he let go.

He spotted the horses grazing underneath a large oak tree, standing alone in the field. He let out a shrill whistle, calling for their attention, but only one raised its head.

Katherine watched as a large white horse, mane flowing marvelously in the wind, galloped excitedly across the field toward them. Snorting wildly, bucking and kicking as it neared where they stood, she wondered if it, too, had intentions to attack. She moved behind Derrick and waited nervously as it came to stand in front of them.

Derrick breathed a sigh as he raised his hands and touched the horse's face. "Nigh, my friend, it is so good to see you," he said as he slid his hands over the stallion's neck and pat him readily. He reached his hand out to Katherine, motioning her to take it. "He's been my faithful companion for as long as I remember."

"He's lovely," she said as she gently patted Nigh's neck, but daring to continue their argument.

Derrick eyed the bottom of her dress. "I don't think you'll be able to ride properly in your long dress."

He knelt down and grabbed hold of the bottom. And before she could stop him, he yanked hard, ripping it up the center and exposing her legs to her mid-thigh.

Blushing profusely, she attempted to yell at him for being so aggressive, but she couldn't. He slid his hands up her sides until he was standing rigid before her with his hands on her hips. And then he chuckled, fondling her sensually as he continued up her arms and over her shoulders, making her catch her breath. And when he released her, he turned away, pompously grinning.

Nigh snorted, nodding as Derrick lifted himself onto his back. He reached for her, grasping her hand when she reflexively acknowledged. With a quick pull, he set her in place behind him and pulled her arms around his waist.

"Nigh," he demanded. "Let's go."

The horse started to gait, and Katherine held on for dear life. She found this rather fascinating as they tread through the vast field underneath a crisp blue sky. It was breathtaking. And as she began to enjoy the ride, she relaxed her grip on Derrick's waist.

"Hold on," he said, turning his head slightly, and then kicked Nigh into a gallop.

She loved his scent, a summer fragrance of fresh air and sea, and tried denying her attraction to him. Loving the closeness of their bodies, the way his muscles felt on her arms as she held him. And the way his soft hair tickled her cheek as she pressed her face against his back made her shiver in delight.

Her fingers caressed his stomach as they crossed a cool shallow river, the horse's stomp causing water to splash on her legs. It felt wonderful against her warm skin, for it not only was reaching the heat of mid-day, but her desires for him were running hot.

She suddenly sat rigid, realizing her thoughts had wandered into a direction she hadn't wanted to go. Placing her fingers at his side, she drew back as far as she could. And trying her best to douse her aching need, she concentrated on something more important.

Gunther's words—they floated in her mind. Derrick may have decided to ignore it, but she certainly could not. In fact, there was no other thing she could think about right now—at least it's what she kept telling herself as she pressed her body again close to his.

She felt the black gem clinging against her breast as if it was a part of her. Derrick had no idea she had it, and she was unsure of what he'd do if he found out. But until then, she'd go along with this escapade and try to enjoy it. For if this wasn't a dream as she hoped, than this may very well be her last adventure.

Chapter Twelve

Derrick helped Katherine slide off Nigh, and her feet sank into the shallow water of the river they'd followed all afternoon. The river had ended just at the brink of the most beautiful waterfall she'd ever seen. And though groaning from the ache of the long ride, she stretched and breathed in the vision of a rainbow mist.

He quickly dismounted and waded through the crystal clear water toward the waterfall. She watched him as he took off his shirt and climbed up onto the flat rock beneath the showering streams, washing away the dust and pollen from his body. She could barely resist the urge to join him.

She couldn't deny how sexy he looked, grinning in delight as he drank in the refreshing water, letting it splash over him. She waded further into the river and found herself just below him. The water felt wonderful against her skin as she splashed it over her dusty arms, trying desperately to keep her eyes away from him, but his voice calling out her name was too enticing.

He leaned down with his hand held out for her to take, but she hesitated, contemplating whether to accept his proposal, or go on wading alone. But when he gestured again for her to take his hand, she finally accepted.

He pulled her up on the rock beside him and held her beneath the water, and suddenly she also carried a beaming grin. Exhilarating, the sound of the falls rushing through her ears as she ran her fingers over her wet hair. Without concern for anything but the way he stared at her, she returned with her own look of wonder.

"You're beautiful," he said as he took her by the hand and raised it to his lips.

Her heart skipped as he kissed her wet palm, and their line of communication fell in sync. She realized she was desperate for his touch, his kiss, she ached for it, but then maybe it was just the moment. Here they were, alone, showering together beneath this refreshing waterfall, surrounded by gorgeous scenery. And this man—this strong, handsome man whose destiny belonged to ending her life stood before her with intent to pursue love.

Pulling her hand away from his caressing mouth, she shivered. The grin she bore a moment ago faded into a perplexed frown. And as she stared blankly at him, unsure of the moment, he sighed and turned away, obviously giving up on her. She reflexively caught his arm and stopped him from jumping down off the rock. "I'm sorry," she said, pulling him back around to face her.

"There is never a need for apologies. I understand my place."

He turned to leave her again, but she pulled him back around. She gazed into his eyes, and the seriousness startled even her, but she stood unflinching before him.

She slid her hands up his strong arms, glistening wet and smooth. She felt his broad shoulders in her grasp, and sighed in curious delight as her palms touched his face.

A shiver shot down her spine as he grabbed her around the waist and lifted her up to meet him. She slid her arms around his neck, pressing her body against his, trying to catch her breath, but it was lost.

He leaned down and touched his lips to hers, sending her body into a tremble as he gently massaged her tongue with his. The kiss was amazing, glorious, and downright passionate, as if maybe he truly loved her, but it ended rather abruptly as Nigh whinnied loud.

Kathryn doused her excitement as Derrick jumped from the rock and held out his hand. "Come on," he said, grasping her hands in his. He helped her down quickly and led her into the cave behind the rock they'd just stood on.

Completely hidden in the shadows, they waited. With Derrick's arm around her shoulders, holding her close, she trembled. Not only in fear of what other unusual things she was going to encounter, but the fact it was dreadfully cold inside the cave.

He turned to face her. "I need to go see what spooked Nigh."

"No," she said worriedly. "Stay here with me. Whatever it is, it'll go away."

He gave her a reassuring grin. "Remember," he whispered. "There is nothing I can't handle. You'll be safe here." He lifted her chin with a curled finger and kissed her tenderly on the lips. "I'll be right back."

She watched him leave the cave and wade through the water. He jumped up onto the bank where Nigh stood snorting nervously, and found his shirt as he scanned the edge of the forest.

"You there," he shouted as he made his way into the trees, beyond Katherine's view.

She stood shivering, watching as the sun began to leave the falls, casting an evening shadow over Nigh. Minutes went by without a word from Derrick, and it suddenly became evident that he might not come back for her.

Swallowing down her fear, she left the frigid cave and waded to the bank. Finding a sunlit spot, she sat down in warm dry grass and wrung out her dress.

Nigh came to stand beside her. He lowered his head and gently nudged her shoulder with his nose, as if he was trying to gather her attention.

"What is it?" she whispered as she stood to her feet. "Is it Derrick?"

He nudged her back, pushing her in the direction of the shadows between the trees.

"You want me to go in there?" she asked, knowing the answer as he nudged her again toward them. "Oh, this is just lovely."

The cynical tone in her voice wavered slightly as she began to walk. Glad to see Nigh was following her nonchalantly, she steadied her pace carefully.

Moving branches with her hands, she made her way through, trying to be as quiet as she could, but it just wasn't possible. There were too many dry twigs and sticks on the ground causing snapping sounds every time she took a step. And Nigh's hooves were making things much noisier.

"If I see another troll," she whispered when she saw a hint of light ahead in a clearing. "I'm going to scream."

The sky was darkening from the setting sun, so it wasn't a glow of sunlight. And as she neared the clearing, she found the light of a campfire, surrounded by a series of fallen logs, conveniently placed for seating.

Glancing around the clearing, she found nothing out of the ordinary, and unfortunately, no Derrick. A terrible sense of dread encircled her as she began to step back thinking maybe he'd gone back to the waterfall to find her. She only hoped. But Nigh nudged her again, pushing her out of the trees and into the clearing.

Nigh nodded his head, snorting as he stepped out behind her. He motioned her to keep moving with another nudge of his nose, but this time he pushed a little harder.

"Stubborn," she protested with a huff. "You're just like your owner."

Too cold to argue, with a horse none the less, she made her way into the camp. Cautiously sitting down on one of the logs near the fire, she peered around in the dark. Though she enjoyed the warmth on her skin, she couldn't stop the trembling of her body.

"Hey!" A loud, terribly annoyed manly voice spoke from the shadows.

She quickly stood up and turned to run, but a large hand caught her dress. She let out a blood curdling scream, struggling to move forward as the stranger held on tight, but she wasn't getting anywhere, and her dress was beginning to rip down the back.

"Now wait up missy," the deep voice demanded. "I'm not going to hurt you."

She lost her balance and fell forward, tumbling to the ground right at Nigh's front hooves. Finding him staring at her as if mocking her, he let out a snort, and his ears propped up high.

As she gazed upward, her eyes caught movement just above Nigh's head. With her arm holding up her dress, she stood on her feet and scanned a long thick rope until she caught sight of a net swinging from the branch of a tall tree. And inside it sat Derrick, kicked back as if he lay in a hammock, but looking terribly perturbed.

She quickly turned around to see who had stopped her. And finding a rather burly man sitting at the fire, hands held out for warmth, she sighed. She knew the only way to get Derrick out of the net was to talk to this strange, gloomy looking man, and an unusually large one at that.

As she made her way to the campfire, she noticed night had finally arrived. The stars were magnificently sparkling in the sky, casting the variant of colors she'd seen from the city.

She sat down on the log and heard her dress rip a little farther down to her backside. Rolling her eyes, she let out a perplexed sigh and turned her attention on the frowning giant.

He was completely bald, but had a big tuft of hair sticking out of his plain white T-shirt. The sleeves of his red flannel shirt were rolled up, showing off his rather large hands stuck up in the air like he was preparing to stop a truck. An eye patch covered one of his eyes, but the other was staring at her.

"I'm sorry about your dress," he said in a gruff, but solemn voice. "I don't know my own strength sometimes."

"It's okay," she said. "It was already ruined." She briefly glanced up at Derrick with accusing eyes. Returning her attention to the man, she shivered. She drew closer to the fire and held her free hand up, trying to get warm.

The man sighed. He unbuttoned his flannel shirt and took it off, and when he stood up, her eyes widened. The man was at least ten feet tall, hulking over her as he draped her shoulders with his shirt. He let out a groan when he returned to his log and sat down, glancing up at Derrick with his eye.

"Is he yours?" he asked, and then returned his attention back on her.

"I suppose you can say that."

The corner of his lips curved upward. "He wandered into my camp a little while ago. I recognize him now, but I didn't want to take the chance he'd turned into a thief." He frowned again as he gazed into the light of the fire. "It seems there are more of them these days. Since the goddess left her lair, it's been dangerous around here."

Katherine watched as he stood up and walked away from the fire. She buttoned up the shirt, touching her breast to make sure the gem wasn't lost. And finding it still stuck on her skin, she breathed a sigh of relief.

She peered into the darkness. A loud thud came from the direction the man had walked, and she found he'd released the net Derrick was in.

He joined her, chuckling as he sat back down on the log. "Unbelievable such a small man could make so much noise when he falls."

Derrick held his back, groaning with an ache as he sat down

beside Katherine. He glared at his captor for a moment, twisting and turning his torso as he worked out the kinks.

"My name is Brutus," he said picking up a stick beside his overgrown foot. He stoked the fire and sparks flew up into the air. "Everyone calls me Cyclops around here. At the account I only have one eye."

She always imagined a Cyclops as a giant man-like creature, grotesquely baring only one eye. They'd always been described as troublesome and mean, but this gentle giant held nothing on lore. "I am not a Cyclops," he said seeing her confusion. "Gods forbid if I ever found out I was."

"So he's the one you told me about this morning?" she asked Derrick who'd found the warmth of the fire.

"I suppose he is," he replied with a shrug. "I've only met him once before, and he didn't like me much then either." He glanced down at the flannel shirt and grinned. "A big ogre like him really knows how to treat a lady. I've heard they like to invite women into their campsites, rip off their clothes and offer condolences, only so they can see their breasts."

"Derrick," Katherine said in a scolding tone. "It's wasn't like that at all."

"It was an accident," Brutus argued. "If she hadn't been trying to run from me, she'd still be in her own clothes."

"You're a feisty fellow," Derrick said as he stood on his feet. "You may have her fooled, but I've met my share of your kind." He glanced down at Katherine. "Trust me. There is no eye socket behind his patch. Let me prove it to you."

"Stay back!" Brutus exclaimed as Derrick took a step toward him. "Or I'll tie you back up in the tree."

"Show her!"

"My muscles could use another workout," Brutus said, flexing his hulking physique with a smirk. "I'll tie you to the tree, chop it down and use you as a weight."

"I highly doubt you could catch me."

Brutus stood up and flashed an evil grin. "Care to give it a try?"

"Sit down!" she exclaimed, demanding Derrick with a finger pointed at the log.

He obeyed, grinning in fascination and yet terribly shocked at her sudden outburst. Sitting down, he glanced at Brutus and found he too was stunned and sitting before she turned her finger on him.

"I've had too much adventure for one day," she emphasized. "I haven't had anything to eat since this morning. My rear-end hurts from riding a horse all day. I'm freezing my toes off. My dress is ripped." Angry tears formed in her eyes. "And I'm tired of listening to two self-absorbed men bicker over who is stronger."

She fell back on the log and held her face in her hands, moaning in frustration. With nowhere to sleep but the cold hard ground, it just made her thoughts that much more agonizing.

"I'm sorry, Katherine," Derrick said as he knelt down before her. "We didn't mean to upset you. Did we Brutus?"

"No little missy," he stammered, shaking his head. "I didn't know of your travels, otherwise I would have invited you into my house sooner."

"Your house?" Katherine raised her head and looked at him.

He smiled innocently as he stood up on his feet and nodded his head. "It's just beyond the trees. Come on. I have an extra bedroom, plenty of food, and I even have some wine."

Katherine smiled. *Finally*, she thought, *some hospitality.*

A huge log house showed up like a glorious surprise just at the foot of a hill on a plot of well-groomed land. Prestigiously built by carpenter hands, it showed the builder took extra care in making it as appealing as he could. And with soft lantern lights glowing in the large windows, it looked inviting and comfortable.

"Impressive," she said as Brutus opened the humongous front door.

"I apologize for the height of my belongings, but I am a rather large man. And I rarely get visitors."

She followed him in bracing herself for something spectacular, and it delivered beautifully. With her mouth agape, she skimmed the room with her eyes, feasting on the old wood design of his furniture. Just as care went into the house, so did the same of its necessities.

Large chairs cushioned with wool cloth were set around a stone fireplace. They welcomed Brutus as he sat down and watched her intently as she made her way into the room.

Candle sconces lit the great room, showing off a collection of extravagant paintings of generals and their armies preparing to charge off to war, of ships sailing stormy seas with cannons pointed at each other firing shamelessly, and interestingly enough, serene landscapes of waterfalls and golden fields.

Painted in oils, lifelike and with care, they were outstanding and professional, and could possibly, in her mind, surpass the value of well-known artists.

"Who painted these?" she asked curiously as she eyed one in particular.

Stones, placed in a circle like Stonehenge, were painted beautifully in a meadow of trees and colorful flowers. And a set of stone steps led upward to the focal point where a marvelous being stood beautifully on a round gray pedestal—a unicorn.

Golden tassels intertwined in her white flowing mane and tail. Gallantly standing, a proud and beautiful goddess, so lifelike and unaware of what was to come.

Katherine stood in awe, staring at her. This was her alleged mother no doubt.

"I painted these," Brutus said as he made his way to her side. "This was the last one I finished. She was beautiful wasn't she?"

"Yes," Katherine said sadly as she turned away.

She glanced at Derrick who'd made himself at home on a rather large bear skin rug on the floor. Lying on his side, he watched her intently, worriedly as she sat down in front of him.

"I'll fix us dinner," Brutus said and went to the kitchen. He pulled the poker off the rack beside the open oven and stirred the flames. "I have chicken in the cooking pot with some vegetables from my garden. It is an old recipe that's sure to warm your bones."

"Thank you," Katherine called out, though her bewildered eyes never left Derrick's.

He placed his hand over hers and gazed at her with an arched brow. As if trying to pry out her emotions over seeing her mother's picture for the first time, he looked at her with questioning eyes.

"Are you okay?" he asked in a soothing whisper, palming her cheek lovingly.

She nodded and offered him a smile, though terribly confused. The thought she was the daughter of a unicorn, a goddess of all magic in the universe made her laugh inside. How could she possibly be this person when she felt nothing of magic?

She cracked a smile as Brutus called them to the table. Taking Derrick's hand in hers she lifted herself to her feet and helped him up. The table was large and the chair was high. She felt like a child when she sat down, dangling her legs over the edge, eyeing the largest bowl she'd ever seen.

"I truly am sorry," Brutus said with a chuckle. "It's the smallest dish I have."

"It's okay," Katherine said, terribly amused by it. She picked up her spoon, about as big as a ladle, and sipped on the broth. It was delicious, but of course, she'd been about starved to death.

"I have to be honest," Brutus said with a sigh. "I cannot eat with this thing on. You were right about me all along. It's just I never receive guests because people think creatures like me are disgusting and unintelligent."

"We have never treated your kind with disrespect," Derrick said defensively.

Brutus took off his eye patch and turned his attention on her, showing her the smooth texture of his skin, rather than an empty socket. "Please accept my apology. I just didn't want to frighten you away." He sighed. "Ever since Astar, my love, left me, I've been in this house alone without anyone to talk to."

"Astar?" Katherine asked, finding interest in his story.

"She was my wife. And let me tell you, it's not easy living with a goddess of war, though she had a way of lighting up a room, usually with torches and explosives. But when I met her, I knew she was the only one for me."

"What happened?"

Brutus set his spoon down and sighed, shaking his head in disappointment. "She grew bored. After I built this place for her, she told me it was too serene and she'd rather live in a cave fighting off giant scorpions. So she left me."

"I'm very sorry," Katherine said thinking it an odd reason for someone to leave their loved one.

"I'm fine now. I have my garden and my livestock to tend to."

She wondered what kind of livestock a giant like him had—sheep as big as a truck, or quite possibly a single story house. Possibly the chickens were as large as Derrick's horse.

"We should leave," Derrick said as he jumped down to the floor.

"Leave?" she asked as he helped her to her feet. "But it's dark outside."

"We would have made it to our destination by now if it wasn't for this oaf."

"He's shown us nothing but kindness."

"But you were not strung up in a net for hours."

She didn't have a comeback to his comment, and as his wary tone played in her ears, heeding a warning to keep her reply, if she could think of one, discreet, she knew they should go. And though the warmth of Brutus's house was inviting, she was ready to leave.

She looked at Brutus and graciously presented him a grin. "Thank you," she said as Derrick led her to the front door. "I would be happy to meet you again someday."

"And I you," Brutus murmured, trying to keep broth from dripping from his mouth. It was then she wished she could stay and at least finish her meal.

Chapter Thirteen

The temple in the woods stood ominous, as dark as the night intertwined in Katherine's hair. The shadows moved with her as they tread across the stone steps, built respectfully in bluestone and granite.

Derrick pushed the heavy door open and walked in without regard. He knew this place, and well obviously, as he disappeared into the dark.

Katherine stood staring into nothing for a moment. Had light not appeared inside, she would have trembled, though she'd already found a shiver from the cool night air.

"Here," he said as light from a single orb began to glow over top of his shoulder. A grin caressed his eager face as she willingly accepted his hand, and he pulled her inside and closed the door.

A symphony of orbs magnificently lit the room with golden light as if welcoming them home, but one small orb circled her head, humming excitedly. She knew this was her little friend from the city.

"Hello," she said, greeting it with a smile as it took its place over her right shoulder for a moment, and then rejoined the others near the ceiling.

She gazed at the one large room before her, veiled in vines climbing the walls and ceiling. It oddly felt cozy, just as home should. Four tall columns held up the stone ceiling around a small pyramid of stairs leading to a single platform. And a bed, like the silk covered one in Derrick's house, sat beautifully at the top, surprisingly untainted by dust.

No matter the similarity, she knew she'd seen this temple before. She recognized it from her dreams. Night after night, she'd climbed the same stairs to meet him, only waking before his face became clear. But now, as Derrick stood hand outstretched to her, she knew he was the one.

Never believing in destiny before, she couldn't help but think of it now, just as she accepted his hand once more. A heavy breath escaped her trembling lips as she held back emotional tears.

"This is home, Katherine," he said as he led her to the top of the stairs. "I lived here for many years guarding Koran, and now I will do the same for you."

"I know this place," she confessed, glancing around the room.

"You should," he said as he sat down on the bed. "You were born in this temple."

She eyed him. A curious thing to say after all this time, though she'd never thought to ask him about it. Now here he was, confessing things he should have told her when they met.

"Tell me more about her," she said as she joined him.

It felt wonderful to sit on something soft. Her legs were weary and her head hurt slightly from the inhalation of field dust. The emptiness in her stomach made her throat pucker, but she held her ground hoping he'd talk.

He faced her with an ardent grin. "We should talk about it over something to eat. I hear your stomach grumbling."

"And what could you possibly have to eat here? This is just one big room with a bed on a pedestal." She eyed him curiously. Maybe he had other things in mind when he chose this place, and the thought made her blush.

"I can still feel magic around me, weaker now, but not unmanageable. Besides, Koran taught me the art of summoning in this very room."

He rose from the bed. With a confident stride, he walked to the edge of the stairs and turned around to face her.

"It's been awhile since I've conjured, so bear with me."

Katherine stood on her feet, eager to see what he was going to do. His crooked grin widened as he clenched his fists. It was startling, the way his eyes suddenly blazed the beautiful turquoise sea she so loved. His lowered brows gave him a certain appearance, as if possessed by some dark entity, incredibly handsome. His black hair slowly twisted around his pale face as incandescent blue light engulfed his body, and brightly lit up the room.

Chills swept through her as he began to chant. She sat down, hand to mouth, listening to the sound of his voice. It was deep, but exceptionally beautiful. And she realized this was his native tongue he so boldly warned her about.

"I'm sorry," he said gravely. "I don't mean to frighten you."

She could only shake her head, unable to speak after such an experience.

"It is the only way to conjure." His voice returned to its normal tone. The glow around him began to fade, but magic still pulsed hazy blue light in the space between his outstretched hands.

A platter materialized within the light, white and oblong, and full of the most beautiful fruit she'd ever seen. Grapes as large as cherries looked succulent ripened on the vine. Unblemished apples and pears made her mouth water and her stomach ache as he set it down on the bed beside her.

She grinned with her eyes, and her lips followed in delight. "Is this real?"

Derrick pulled off a plump grape and stuck it in his mouth. "Delicious," he said, eyeing her with a mischievous grin.

He lifted the vine to her mouth and ran a single grape across her dry lips. Mischievous indeed, she thought as she opened her mouth and let him drop one on her tongue.

She smiled in pleasure. "Do you know any more wonderful tricks?"

"A few," he replied, returning with his own gratifying grin. "Magic comes from everything around us—trees, grass, the water, and even in the air you breathe. The smallest organism holds a power you can only imagine, but it takes years to learn how to draw it out without taking its entire essence."

"Do you know how to conjure clothes?" she asked, glancing down at the overly large flannel shirt. She unbuttoned it and opened it to reveal her tattered dress, hanging loosely below her neckline, and ripped from the bottom a little too close for comfort.

"No," he answered, moving close to her as he eyed her peculiarly. "What is this?" He touched her softly along the neckline, swiping a lock of her hair from her neck.

She followed his eyes to the small lump showing through her dress. Panic suddenly encompassed her as she rose from the bed and stepped back with a scowl. But he followed, leaving his curious eyes on her chest.

"I'm offended," she said.

"Excuse me for being overly blunt, but that is not your nipple." He backed her down the steps. His heated eyes were suddenly on hers, wanting to hear her speak the truth. "What are you hiding from me?"

"I'm not hiding anything."

He grasped the cloth tightly in his hands and quickly pulled it apart. The dress ripped open, exposing the black diamond on her right breast.

"If you want to look at me, you only have to ask," she said in hopes it would deter his oncoming fury, but she knew his temperament.

His eyes widened, brows arched and then lowered into a scowl as he gazed at the gem. He took a step back as if he'd been slightly shoved, causing him to briefly lose his balance.

She watched him carefully, as he cautiously began to pace, obviously thinking about this predicament as he rubbed his jaw with his hand. She could tell he was terribly angry, but surprise and shock lingered with him.

"To fathom you have carried the gem in your possession all this time." He breathed out in astonishment. "I spent three days begging my father for it. He nearly killed me, Katherine! And yet you stand here before me holding it?"

"I'm sorry," she said as she carefully peeled the gem off her skin. The odd adhesive caused discomfort and left a painful red mark. "I was afraid of what you'd do if you found out."

"What I would do?" he asked through clenched teeth. "You can't begin to understand!"

"Calm down," she said, wanting it to be a demand, but it came out weak and frightful. "It's not a big deal." She held the gem in her palm. "If it's any consolation, I never wanted it back." She held it out to him. "Here, I'm giving it to you now."

Do not let it leave your grasp. She remembered what the shadow had told her. But why—why would he say such a thing? Questions ran through her mind, but only if someone would pull her away from the dark and answer them. She closed her palm and clenched it tight in her fist, oddly glad he hadn't taken it from her.

Though he still paced angrily, her demeanor fell flat as she made her way back to the bed. She was too tired for this. The day had been long, and the fruit on the platter was too inviting to pass up any longer, so his outburst was something he'd have to deal with on his own.

She sat down and began to eat. Ah, but it was good. Either she was so hungry it didn't matter what she ate, or it was ultimately the best fruit she'd ever had. With juice dripping down her chin, she indulged in the moment. Closing her eyes, she blocked out his image drawing near. She ignored his worried voice asking her how she could eat at such a moment. And it didn't make any difference if he screamed, even in the same manner as Mila, she wasn't going to listen.

"Katherine!" he yelled as he seized her shoulders and shook her, but she kept eating the fruit from the tray.

Nothing—no word or motion accepted his proposal to listen. He didn't deserve her attention, not even in his demand. Not his eyes glowing beautifully, angrily. Nor the way he shook her, mild, but brazen enough to make the platter of fruit fall from her lap and scatter across the floor.

Loose grapes rolled, stopping just short of the steps. Tears came to her eyes as she watched one bounce its way down to floor level, and then another follow in its path.

"How did you get it?" he asked urgently, shaking her again and finally drawing her eyes to his.

She opened her hand and gazed at the perfect gem, ignoring his tightening grasp. It looked so small, so ridiculously like a simple black rock ready to be tossed into the sea. Not even the slightest hint of danger emitted off it, so how in the world could it hold such a terrible power?

"It's just a simple rock," she said in a soft whispering voice. "It was left with me by my parents when I was an infant. I never knew them."

Derrick loosened his grip. The anger he'd portrayed suddenly lifted into a bewildered poise as he watched tears stream down her pale cheeks.

"Please, tell me how it came to you," he said in a calmer voice.

She glanced at him blankly and replied. "Take it." She held it out to him, hoping he'd take it and end this terrible nightmare. The truth was she didn't want it anymore. To be rid of it would be her ultimate goal, a cleansing, so to speak. And though it had meant so much in her life at one time, it meant nothing now.

"Take it!" she demanded, wiping tears from her cheeks, finding her verve, or quite possibly her wits end. "Just take it and do whatever you have to."

She forced open his hand, meaning to place the jewel in his palm, but it managed to cling to her skin.

"It's a sign," he said as he watched her desperately try to remove it from her hand. "The jewel doesn't want to come to me. It belongs to you."

"Stop talking so poetic," she scowled as she picked at it with her fingernail.

"I can't help but find humor in this," he said chuckling as she became terribly frustrated.

"I don't understand," she said gritting her teeth. "It easily came off earlier."

"This was before you decided to give it away." He grasped her fingers and rolled her palm. "No more secrets, Katherine," he said in a serious manner.

"Secrets?" she asked curiously.

"No words we speak here will find curious ears. And no eyes will linger on us, not in my temple."

"What do you mean?" she asked, suddenly feeling rather vulnerable.

He glanced upward in brief annoyance and then sighed. "The gods watch us, and they listen to everything we say. They collaborate to make sure we don't come together, though they are doing a very lousy job."

Though terribly confused, she watched him, hoping he would enlighten her. But all he did was toss her a fleeting look as if waiting for an answer, and she knew exactly what it was.

Glancing down at the gem on her palm, she sighed. "Some dark thing brought it to me and said it was from the Ferryman. He told me I should never let it go."

"A dark soul," he whispered with unease. "This is very strange."

An insecure moment hit her when the words rolled off her lips. Unsure of what he'd think, she kept her stare from leaving the gem in her palm.

Finding control in her voice, she finally raised her tired eyes to his. "He came when you were away at sea."

"He must have stolen it from the lair while I kept Poseidon busy.

The ship bearer is the only mortal soul in direct contact with your father. It only makes sense to send a messenger." Realizing he'd just slipped out information he hadn't wanted to give, he shifted nervously as a perplexed look engaged her face.

"Who's my father?" she asked, grasping his shirt in both hands as she stared into his eyes, pleading.

"I ..." he stammered. "I cannot say—not yet."

"But nobody can hear us," she emphasized, feeling her eyes blur with tears. "I swear I'll never mention it again. Just please, I need to know."

"Katherine," he said, trying to pull away from her, but she held fast to his shirt. "I'm sorry."

"You don't trust me," she whispered somberly.

He grasped her shoulders gently. "I trust you," he declared with a sigh. "With all the will in my body, I want to tell you the truths you seek, but I cannot, not until the proper time comes."

"But you're supposed to be my guide," she replied softly. "And right now, I'm terribly lost."

His perplexed emotions were written in his worried eyes and on his softening face as he pulled her into his arms and pressed his lips to her temple. "There is truth in your words," he whispered. "More than you know."

She pulled back from his tender embrace and gazed upward, catching his heartfelt stare. "What am I supposed to do?"

"You're supposed to forget about all you have come to know about your unwanted destiny. You're supposed to feel safe as I guard you with my life here in this temple. I'll give you everything you desire. My heart, my soul ..." He slid his hand over her blushing cheek, thumbing a tear. "And I will give you my body, if you will have me."

Silence followed his last words and his eyes ignited into a yearning flame. Sliding his fingers through her hair made her skin chill with sudden desiring passion.

Her breath was lost when his lips touched hers, swiftly engulfing her in an emotion worthy of exhilaration. Guilty pleasure pushed her tears away as he leaned her back on the bed, arousing an ache for him to touch her in places to make her sigh.

She wanted him, though the dismissal of unspoken truths lingered on her troubled mind. But the way he touched her, softly caressing her skin as he worked off her torn garment dizzied her serious thoughts.

"Let go of your worry," he said, kissing her softly on the lips. He enjoyed the prickle of her skin as he pulled his fingers across her breast, across the small red mark where the jewel used to hide. "Allow me to help you forget, at least for a little while."

She slid her hands over his broad shoulders, feeling his muscles tense as he exposed his naked body to her. With his hair mingling in his beautiful eyes, he looked upon her as if she were a goddess. Her sensations were immense as he pressed his warm body to hers and lay hard against her stomach. The ache for him urgently rose.

He kissed her, gently pressing his tongue to hers as the magic surrounding them rolled off their bodies. The excess of need coveted them with pleasurable desires, bursting in tension. Blue flames licked them, caressed them, and filled them with relentless craving.

He shifted his hips and positioned himself over her. She was ready to accept him with open arms and surrender to the ecstasy of love making. And at last, it happened.

In one sudden gentle thrust, he filled her void, making her lose her breath. A sigh broke from her lips and her body tingled in pleasure.

His body was strong as he moved against her, but only touching his lips lightly on her neck, pulling at her skin, and slowly making his way to her breast. The tickle of excitement showed as he pressed his warm tongue against her nipple, sending her into a blissful moan.

As his thrusts grew to a steady pace, every deep thought she'd endured in her unworldly journey left her mind. And nothing but the love they were sharing encumbered her, and surrounded her with an urge to cry out in glorious rapture.

Sliding her arms around his neck, she pulled her body up to meet his. Every exciting thrust, every moaning sigh brought her closer until he broke out into a pant.

His body stiffened against her. She threw her head back, joining him in the moment of breaking tension as he hit her spot, sending her into a fit and releasing pleasure inside her.

He fell into her arms, breathing heavily onto her neck. And she held him, wanting to stay there forever. She wanted to forget where she was, though not who she was with. For he was the man of her dreams, the one true being who could show her what life truly was, and what secrets their future would hold.

A loud crash of stone against stone quickly sobered her thoughts and her orgasmic sensation. Her deeply embedded thoughts of sharing her life, hiding away forever with him in this temple, immediately dissipated.

Bliss turned into a frantic scramble to see what was causing such a commotion. And as the front door stood open wide, a cold wind flooded the temple.

She shivered as she caught sight of a group of people standing in the doorway ominously dressed in black, and conveniently hooded to hide their identity. They quickly entered the orb-lit room as if floating on the breeze itself. A dark, sinister whirlwind carried them to the bottom of the steps, but they made no further advance.

"What is this?" Derrick yelled in a rage as he quickly lifted his body from Katherine. "You dare enter my temple without invitation!"

Two cloaked individuals stayed at the bottom stair, but the other three began to walk toward him. Their footsteps tread silently as if their feet never touched the ground, but Katherine could see plain as day a pair of dark shoes beneath the leader's cloak. Her eyes widened. For it wasn't the feet of a man she was watching, but that of a woman.

Derrick quickly clothed himself to his waist, eyes blazing as the woman made her way up the steps toward him. A ball of fiery red light materialized in his right hand—a defensive magic, unbound and ready to be hurled at the intruders.

"Stop at once," a woman's voice implored, her breath erratic as if she'd run miles to get there. "You cannot give in to your desires!"

The voice sounded oddly familiar to Katherine as she covered herself with the sheet. As she came to stand behind Derrick, she blushed, feeling terribly awkward for them getting caught in such a moment. She peered around his shoulder, but just enough to get a glimpse of who was speaking to them.

"Who are you to make such demands?" Derrick asked lowering the magic he'd conjured to a candle's flame.

The woman stopped before him and lifted her head. She pushed back the hood exposing black hair, glistening with sweat from the long journey she'd obviously taken. And when she pulled her long strands back from her face, she revealed strikingly familiar blue eyes.

"I'm too late," she said, dropping to her knees in a solemn mourn.

Derrick stepped back in shock, a perplexed fascination for how this could be. He turned to find Katherine standing behind him, holding a similar expression, but her face was as pale as a ghost.

Katherine couldn't believe what she was seeing. Like looking in a mirror, here she was, standing before them. And obviously by the way she acted, something terrible was going to happen.

But at the moment, it didn't matter. The only important thing was having Derrick near, catching her as she fell forward into unconsciousness. For the vision of her self standing there was just too much to endure.

•

"I took a big risk coming here," Katherine confessed as she closed the front door and then joined him on the steps. "It has been so long since I have spoken to anyone outside the river."

When she looked at Derrick with pleading eyes, he could see the difference between her and the Katherine still lying unconscious on the bed. This one was slightly older, and had a subtle hint of exhaustion and grief.

He could see a struggle within her, desperately reaching out for his help, though uncertainty lingered in her glance, as if she was somehow forced into coming here. He wanted to oblige, but something was keeping him from doing so.

"Who are they?" he asked curiously.

She turned to the individuals still standing in the doorway, cloaked as if in hiding. "They are passing souls interrupted by magic unbound by Atlantean laws. They are unstoppable, for they hold no substance. And now they are his soldiers, sent to destroy everything and everyone in Atlantis." She gazed into his eyes, pleading for him to understand, but he saw discrepancy hinted inside them. "My true fate lies in your hands. You must take me to the pyramid."

Derrick breathed an aggravated sigh, brushing off her ridiculous words. "You know nothing of fate. I will not sacrifice you."

"Did you truly believe you could hide from him here?" She grabbed him by the hand and gathered her words carefully, eyeing the cloaked figures around her. "My father told me what is to happen."

"You spoke with him?" Derrick asked, arching curious brows. Though he was thoroughly confused by this visit, he decided to play along with whatever game she was playing.

"He instructs them to extend the black river into the world of the living. For he is raging war, wanting to end Zeus's reign and control everything in the universe. And in order to do that, he must have the gem."

"There has to be a way to stop him."

"The diamond holds more than you can ever imagine—secrets even the gods know nothing about." She eyed him gravely. "There is one other way but to take me to the rift at the pyramid."

The hooded figure beside her suddenly took hold of her arm, as if reminding her what her mission was. She nodded in agreement, but eyed Derrick in silent plea.

She knelt down before him and covered his hands with hers. With a quaint grin, she gently grasped them. "Take me to the rift and push me through," she whispered. "Pull the gem from my hand as you speak the words of time."

He glanced at her curiously. "I need more time to figure this out."

"There is no time!" She rose to her feet with a scowl, but eased her brow when she saw his conflict. "The true child is unaware of his destiny."

The dark figures began to pull her back as if she'd said too much, but she managed to free herself, eyeing them angrily. They backed away, oddly bowing in forgiveness.

Derrick's eyes came to rest on his Katherine, still lying in bed, sleeping peacefully, wholly unaware. A goddess of destruction— how could he not have known? How could he not sense such a disturbing secret? But even this Katherine didn't emanate such power. It was much different, as if she were another being altogether.

"What of the actual horn?" he asked, returning his suspicious glance to her intent blue eyes. "If it held no magic, then why did Koran die?"

"I was her guide into heaven." She eyed the oncoming figures once again threatening to intervene. "It is not important," she continued as she stood up with a defeated sigh.

"By this time tomorrow, an army will swarm through Atlantis, bringing with them ultimate destruction. They will end lives quickly, creating more of his soldiers. You must end my life and release the magic into the world. Only then will darkness be stopped and the souls will no longer be held captive."

Derrick sat, appalled by her contradicting words. He shook his head in disbelief. Even though it came from this so-called Katherine, it just wasn't convincing enough, and knowingly so by the odd look in her eye.

"You refuse," she said, grinning ominously.

"You speak in tongues." Derrick shook his head and rose to his feet. He stepped up to the bed and gathered his sleeping Katherine in his arms.

"You will see," she said as she pulled the hood back over her head. "Tomorrow will be the end. If you ignore my warning, our souls will rest on your shoulders for eternity."

Derrick's body glowed magnificently, an immediate burst of magic. He ignored the pleading look in her eyes, and concentrated on where he wanted to go, to his home in Atlantis. And with an explosion of power, they ignited inside the flames, and suddenly disappeared.

Katherine pushed her hood back once more and looked upward, concern written on her face. Hoping her words were sincere enough, and he hadn't heard her whispers, she sighed as she opened the front door.

"I did as you asked," she said. "Now please, release the spirits as you promised."

A moment of silence passed. Either he hadn't heard, or didn't want to. But when the orbs began to gather, creating a wide blackened circle along the ceiling, she knew he was about to speak.

"He does not believe you," a deep whispering voice eerily spoke from the circle.

"He will when tomorrow comes," she replied, bowing her head slightly as her voice deepened, and the image of Katherine faded into a dark substance. "There is still time. He will see death and realize what he must do. My words will haunt his ears, and your reign will be complete once he releases the magic."

"You betray me yet again. And now you will leave my river and follow them. No souls will pass until the magic is released to me."

The cloaked figure drifted toward the front door as the others gathered around, moaning eerily as the dark whirlwind they arrived on picked them up and carried them out into the shadows of the night.

Chapter Fourteen

"Wake up!" Katherine heard Derrick shout. A light touch on her face sent her eyelids into a flutter. He shook her mildly, but stern enough to gather her unsteady attention.

In a haze of waking she heard screaming, women and children in unbridled fear, voices shrill with panic. Shouts from men, angry and overburdened by the capture of loved ones, came from outside the house.

An explosion roared in her ears, followed by the sound of breaking, crumbling stone. She sat up in sudden panic, covering her ears until the ringing went away.

"What's going on?" she cried as Derrick quickly pulled her out of bed and just in time for her to see a large ball of fire hurtle past the open window. "Derrick!" she yelled frantically, terribly bewildered as he pulled her to the far end of the room and pushed her against the wall.

He positioned her behind him, shielding her with his body, protecting her from whatever was outside. "We need to get you out of here," he said, glancing back to find fear in her tear-filled eyes. "Listen to me," he continued, taking hold of her arms. "He is looking for the gem."

"Who is?" she asked, cringing as another explosion roared in her ears.

"There is no time for questions," he urgently replied as the outer wall of his house collapsed.

He grasped her hand tight and led her to the opening. They carefully peered around the corner of broken stone before leaving on quick feet, hoping nobody would spot them.

Katherine couldn't fathom what was going on. As he guided her toward the center of the city, pausing to duck under open windows or hide behind blasted walls, she tried to remember.

She barely heard his demand to stay put as he leaned around the corner to check the main walkway. Thoughts of making love to him in the temple jostled her last memory as if the explosion in the near distance set it off.

They'd been interrupted, by her alleged future self. She'd broken down on the steps, claiming she had come too late. But what had she meant? Had she come through a time rift just to stop them from being together? It didn't make any sense.

Derrick grabbed her hand and pulled her out onto the walkway behind him. She kept her eyes on her feet as they fled toward the pyramid, but her heart suddenly dragged the ground with an anchoring result.

Tears blurred her vision as she gasped in horror, completely appalled as she stopped, hand to mouth, witnessing all the bodies lying dead at her feet. Strung out down the walkway, bleeding and broken, their mouths left open in terror. Her stomach began to ache, and nausea worked to the back of her throat.

"Don't look at them!" Derrick shouted as he grasped her hand and pulled her with him. "There's no time to mourn for them now!"

She cried, plain and simple. But these Atlanteans she'd come to know as kind souls deserved more than her solemn tears. They deserved mourning from their gods, from the ones who was supposed to watch over them and protect them from their enemies.

Wiping tears with her free hand, she glanced around. There had to be some clue, some sort of symbol this army carried to confirm their identities. Would she know them when she found out?

She needed time to figure out her thoughts, to figure out what was going on, and what they were going to do. And her chance finally came when Derrick stooped at the end of the street. The pyramid wasn't far, and he obviously had intentions of getting her there, but she wasn't ready to move any farther.

She eyed the small stone dwelling on the other side of the street. Though it was slightly damaged, the front door was partially hidden by broken stone from the house next door. It was dark inside, enough that a quick glance wouldn't arouse curiosity.

With a sudden rush of courage, she pulled her hand away from

Derrick's and ran across the street. Her heart pumped fast as she leapt over the broken stone in the doorway, and fell inside the darkness, clutching her heaving chest.

As she tried to catch her breath, Derrick jumped in behind her. He quickly grabbed her up and covered her mouth with his hand. They quietly and carefully stepped back against the wall just as three darkly cloaked figures floated by.

"Atlantis is no more," Derrick said angrily as he slid down the wall, palming his forehead. "I failed to keep it alive."

"It's my fault," Katherine whispered. "I wasn't supposed to live, and this is the result of my selfishness."

He grabbed her tightly by the arms, but released them almost immediately. "I don't ever want to hear you say that again!"

"It's true," she replied, wiping tears from her cheeks and catching his worried eyes. "It's not too late, Derrick. You can still stop this from happening."

He frowned as she raised her palm to show him the black jewel, emphasizing with a gesture for him to take it, but his eyes wouldn't leave hers.

The explosions finally died down, giving their moment an odd silence, until Derrick sighed. He lowered his eyes to the gem in her palm, knowing what he had to do.

"We have to make it to the top of the pyramid," he said somberly. "It is the only chance we have." Her heart suddenly dropped as he grasped her hand. He pulled her against him and held her close, stroking her hair. "You are the bravest woman I've ever known."

Another moment of silence went by as he held her. But his words gave her the strength to pull from his embrace and stand up with an outstretched hand.

"Let's get this over with," she said.

"It's not far," he whispered, glancing down the walkway to make sure it was empty.

He eyed the pyramid, listening intently for a sign the enemies had moved on. An explosion went off in the distance, letting him know they were somewhat safe to move out.

"Wait," Katherine said, catching his attention before he led her out in the open.

"What is it?" he asked curiously.

She arched her brow. "Since I'm going to die in a few moments, the least you can do is tell me who my father is. I think I have a right to know."

Puzzlement spread over him like wildfire. She could tell he was struggling with an inner voice to either tell her the truth, or shrug it off like he had before. She only hoped he'd comply and give her the information she desired.

"You'll meet him soon," was all he could say as he pulled her out the door.

I'll meet him soon? But her thoughts immediately faded as they began running up the steps of the pyramid. *This is it.*

Her final walk, or run at the moment, was at hand. Her clock would stop and her soul would fly away to the heavens. Maybe she'd even meet her mother in passing, for it was indeed a restoration of her life. And all the inhabitants of Atlantis would swing back to the living. It was a strange sentiment, but one to ease her weary mind and accept this terrible fate.

When they reached the top, Derrick swung her around to face him. He caressed her shoulders lovingly as his eyes began to glow beautifully.

"We will meet again soon," he said in a confident breath as he placed an object in her palm. "Do as the dark soul instructed and it will change the fate you have seen here. Take the orb with you, for it will guide you back to me."

"I don't understand," she said, completely stupefied by his words.

"You will."

With a curious glance, she watched him as he began to speak in the same dark manner as when he'd conjured the platter of fruit. She desperately wanted to know what he meant, but she had no time to stand there and dwell on it as a group of cloaked soldiers made their way toward them.

"Hurry!" Katherine exclaimed without another thought. "Draw out the horn and take my life before it's too late!"

Derrick continued to chant, but much faster now. He glowed as if he were a star, shining in the night sky, lighting the corner of Katherine's eyes as she watched their enemies draw forth fire, shouting for them to stand still.

Derrick's chanting suddenly stopped. With a stern grasp, he pulled her around to face him with his back to their enemies.

Seriousness surrounded him, and a sense of urgency intensified his colorful aura—a temporal sea.

The beauty around him flourished like the sun's rays hitting the deep, unbridled ocean. He was her savior, her guide, and the man she loved more than life itself, and the eagerness to die for him hit her heart like a million daggers. Love poured from her body, her mind, and her soul as in one final motion, she lifted herself to meet him in a kiss.

The way he returned her embrace was unconditional, and held a yearning to fulfill every desire, living through every year they could have spent together in one brief moment of passion, and in one incredible kiss.

But it had to end, for they separated, ready to say goodbye. Her death was imminent, untimely and unfortunate. And as he walked her to the highest platform, she saw tears forming in his eyes, crying for her, and with her.

"I love you, Katherine," he said as he took her by the hands and grasped them gently. "Remember this always as you walk away. Never turn back as you journey through time and change our destinies."

At first she wasn't sure what he was talking about, but when she turned to find he'd walked her into the time rift, she began to panic.

"Wait!" she urged as he quickly shoved her inside.

She fell on her backside, watching in horror as the rift began to close her inside. She held her hand out to him. "This isn't the way it's supposed to end!"

"It's too late," he said in confidence.

"Then come with me!" she yelled, reaching as far as she could, hoping she'd grab hold of him, but he was too far away.

"I cannot," he replied in a muffled voice as he turned to face the dark soldiers. He stood proud, bold, and ready to face his undeniable conclusion.

"Get out of there," Katherine screamed as she reached for him again, tears streaming her face. "Please, take my hand!"

As if he'd become a holographic portrait, her hands moved through him. Trying desperately to touch him, to pull him away from their hands of fire, she frantically cried as she only touched the clouds causing a misty trail to swirl around her rigid fingers.

She watched them release their fire, and a cloud of smoke permeated the air. Her vision blurred as he became engulfed in flames, burning as he fell to his knees, and then to the ground.

"No," she cried, furiously grasping for something solid, but she could only touch emptiness.

She was distraught as his ashes flew into the sky, and the image of his lifeless body faded into the clouds, leaving her completely alone. The lingering vision made her ill with sadness, and the horrifying burden on her heart sent her into complete shock.

Death was her destiny, not his. How could she go on knowing he was dead, and believing she was the cause of ending his life and his world?

Through blurry eyes, she glanced down at the ocean beneath her. Too upset to feel fear, she stood up on her feet and began to walk, uncaringly stepping toward the mirror of familiar stones, the opening to her ordinary world.

A numbing sensation coursed through her as she stepped through and fell to solid ground beneath the large stone doorway— the same one they'd traveled through at the beginning of their journey.

Voices came clear but her eyes were too swollen to look into their stunned faces. Tourists, no doubt in wonder at the beauty and mystery of these precious stones, believed a fallen angel lay at their feet. A heart-broken, tear-stricken angel filled with remorse and shame that she was glad to be alive.

Chapter Fifteen

Remember my words. His voice, his beautiful, profound voice came to her again, haunting her even as she lay in the grass gazing up into a cloudless sky. As if he spoke into her ear through the whispering wind, it relaxed her, but only for a moment.

Tears instantly flooded her eyes, for she knew he was gone. She'd seen it happen just hours before, and she could do nothing but watch. And as she lay in the field next to her beloved Stonehenge, she wished she could go back and save him.

She sat up, terribly disoriented. It was her first move since she'd rose from the stone doorway and stumbled out into the field. For the most part, the tourists had left her alone, except for a few lingering eyes perhaps speculating she was a drunk with nowhere else to go. If only she was, maybe the pain wouldn't be so difficult to manage.

She'd lain there for hours it seemed, but it may have been the entire day. She hadn't been able to clear her mind from seeing her lover die a horrible death, at least not until now as she glanced around at her surroundings.

The sun was sinking toward the horizon. She stood up on shaky legs, trying desperately to hold back more tears, but they fell as she made her way across the circle. Ignoring the few stares she received, she found the path, eager to get to her car, but she suddenly came to a halt.

She breathed a disgruntled sigh, glancing down to see if, by chance, he'd stuck her car keys in a pocket. But unfortunately there were none in the simple white gown he'd dressed her in.

Funny she hadn't paid any attention to it. The last thing she remembered was being wrapped in a sheet, naked underneath, and basking in an afterglow. The memory made her find a short smile, but it quickly faded back into a frown when she realized she'd also lost the orb he'd carefully placed in her palm.

"Where is it?" she asked aloud in a scratchy, panicky voice. Glancing around, she hoped she'd spot it, but when she also found the empty space her car used to be in, tears welled in her eyes.

"This doesn't seem to be your day now does it?" asked a pleasant English voice from inside a nearby car.

She turned to find a man dressed in a white T-shirt and jeans sitting in an old yellow Mini-Cooper with the window rolled down. He blew cigarette smoke from his mouth, dangling his elbow over the window sill as he tossed her an attentive grin.

Though he was an older, handsome gentleman, his impression was young, confident, and definitely in fine shape by the look of his arms. He flashed his bright blue eyes with a smile and motioned with his head for her to move closer.

"Listen," he said as he doused his cigarette in the ash tray. "You're obviously lost. I can give you a ride to the nearest town if you like. It's not too far of a walk, but night's coming. And I imagine walking alone in the dark is not your forte."

There were so many things wrong with this picture. A man sitting alone in a parking lot, offering to give a lone woman a ride somewhere was just a tad suspicious, but he seemed oddly familiar. Still, what did she have to lose, when she'd already lost everything she held dear?

"I have to find something I lost first," she said, turning away to go search for it, but he stopped her with his voice.

"Is this what you're looking for?" he asked, holding up the orb Derrick had given her. "It dropped from your hand when you fell, but I saved it before someone decided to steal it from you."

She took it from his grasp and eyed him curiously. "Thanks."

"Hop in," he said with a grin. "I promise I won't bite," he added as he started his car, watching her cautiously walk around the front to the passenger side.

She settled into the seat and reached for the seatbelt. With a wary smirk, she snapped the buckle into place. Nervousness overwhelmed her and her lips began to tremble slightly.

"I can tell you don't hitch rides often," he said as he threw the car into gear and sped off onto the highway. "Not to worry, Miss. I'm one of the nicest strangers you'll ever meet." He grinned at her as he sheathed his eyes with dark sunglasses and then reached down to turn on the radio. "So what kind of music do you like? Whatever it is, I probably own it." He chuckled. "You can say I'm a fanatic. Blues, rock, heavy metal, classical. I've even been known to listen to a little bit of country and rap."

"That's nice," she replied, minding her manners though she wasn't in the mood for talk.

All she wanted to do was sit there and cry, but for some reason, she couldn't do it in front of him. He was just too easy, and it was contagious, not only because of his friendly voice and buoyant smile, but from the lovely warm wind blowing in from the open sunroof.

"So do you live around here?"

"It's none of your business," she replied with a snap, gathering his immediate attention.

"I'm sorry. I didn't mean to pry." He returned his glance to the road. "I just figured you'd like to talk about your troubles."

"You figured wrong," she said as she fumbled her orb that for some reason refused to glow.

Her last word seemed to linger through the car. And he became terribly quiet, maybe afraid to say anything else for fear he'd get his head bitten off again.

"I like your car," she said, hoping it'd mend the situation. "I like the older style better than the new one."

He nodded his head with a sudden spark in his eye. "You and I both," he replied. "I love the classics. They're easy to work on, but the parts are incredibly hard to find. Just last year I put together a 1969 Rover TC. Found it at an old man's farm, sitting in an overgrown hay field. It'd been there for thirty years," he said with a genuine laugh.

She smiled, feeling a little more at ease. She even began to listen to the music playing on the CD player—an instrumental.

"I've heard this song before, on the plane when I moved here," she said, but the look he gave her made her feel like she'd said something wrong.

"You've heard this before?" he asked, returning his uneasy eyes to the road.

"Yes," she replied curiously. "But the song I heard had words."

"Well," he said, clearing his throat nervously. "You couldn't have heard this particular one because it's not out yet."

"Yes it is," she argued. "I remember it."

"And how long ago was this?"

"I don't know," she thought for a moment. "Maybe a year."

"A year?" he asked with a chuckle, terribly amused. "Prove it to me by singing the end."

She eyed him curiously, unsure of what his intentions were. Did he really want to hear her terrible out of tune voice? Or was he completely insane?

"I've only heard it once."

"The ending sentence should be easy enough to remember then," he retorted. "You don't have to sing it. Just say the words."

What a strange request, she thought, terribly puzzled by this charming man. But as they pulled into a small gas station and parked, she sighed in relief.

He took off his shades. "I'm waiting," he urged as he rested his palm on the top of the steering wheel, staring at her with bright gracious eyes.

She watched the strands of his short black hair blow gently in the breeze, but her eyes wandered to the phone booth in the distance. "And I will never forget you," she said, her voice wavering slightly as her cheeks turned a shade of rose. "Thank you for the ride ... what was your name?"

"Ian," he said, filling in her emphasis.

"Thank you, Ian."

Ignoring his dazed glance, she left the car and walked toward the phone. He was a might strange, this one, but so convenient to be there when she needed someone. She was truly thankful.

She dialed Ty's number, and couldn't wait to hear his voice. It had felt like years since she'd talked to him. Honestly, she wasn't sure how long it'd been since she'd left the museum, but when she heard his voice answer the phone, it didn't matter anymore.

"Ty," she said, bursting into tears. "I'm so relieved you're home. I really need you right now."

"Who is this?"

"Katherine," she replied, wiping tears from her cheeks.

"Katherine," he said in a detached tone. "I don't know a Katherine."

"What are you talking about? We work at the museum

together."

A brief pause, and then she heard him sigh. "Listen," he continued. "I understand my work generates a bit of controversy here and there. And on occasion, it probably deserves the criticism it gets by activists, I'm sure such as yourself. But please refrain from dialing my personal number. If you have a complaint, then please tele the museum."

The phone clicked. Katherine stood astonished not only because he'd hung up on her, but because he'd totally blew her off like he didn't know her at all. Was he really that angry with her?

Puzzled, she turned to find Ian, still sitting in his car, fingers to his mouth with obviously something on his mind. He stared at her, quite possibly with the same glazed look she carried as she left the phone booth terribly bewildered.

Unsure of what to do, she stood hugging her arms as the chill of dusk hit her bare skin. Ian eyed her, but didn't say a word until she walked toward the station's front door.

"Is your ride on the way?" he called out, stopping her before she reached the entrance.

She wasn't sure what to say, but the truth was disheartening, and terribly lonely. "I don't think he remembers me," she said nervously, feeling a little embarrassed. It was such a strange thing to say, but she couldn't muster up a lie at the moment. Tears had sprung in her worried eyes as she stood shivering.

Ian stepped out of his car and walked to her. And before she could stop herself, she fell into his arms and cried.

"I have a spare room at my house if you'd like to stay," he said softly. "You can sort out whatever it is you're going through there."

She nodded, trying to straighten her face as he led her to the car and helped her in with a guiding hand. And in no time, they were back on the road, heading in the other direction.

•

Katherine followed Ian up the front steps of his single-story home. It was beautiful, nestled in tall trees presenting serenity worth retiring in. But she was too tired, and too upset to admire her surroundings.

"I'm sorry about the mess," he said as he turned the living room light on, revealing a cozy, very well decorated room. "I work from home, so it's kind of a double disaster."

He grinned nervously as he removed filled staff paper from his soft suede couch, creating a space for her. "Please," he said, gesturing for her to sit down. "I'll start a fire."

She sunk down into the couch. It had been too long since she'd felt something so soft beneath her, other than the bed her and Derrick made love in.

She felt guilty—guilty for being alive, and guilty for causing his death by leading an unseen enemy into his world. It had only happened this morning, but here she was, feeling warmth from a stranger's fire, sitting on soft furniture, and furthermore, being cared for. She didn't deserve this.

Tears stung her eyes as she stared at the slowly rising flames in the fireplace. A flashback of magical fire suddenly blazed inside her, and her heart dove at the vision of his ashes.

"You're crying again," Ian said, noticing streaming tears on her peaked face. "I'm a good listener if you want to talk about it."

Unable to tear her eyes from the fire and look at him, she answered in a daze. "You wouldn't believe me if I tried."

He sat down on the hearth, eagerness emitting off his stare. "I've seen things in my lifetime you wouldn't believe. So I'm sure your story is quite plausible. You just need to trust me."

She finally looked at him with lowered brows. "Trust you?" she asked in a rebellious tone. "I don't even know you. I don't know why I'm even here."

He nodded in concurrence as he rested his elbows on his knees. He clasped his fingers together and bowed his head in thought. "Well, you trusted me enough to come to my home. I think it's a good sign you need a shoulder. And by the tears in your eyes, it's obvious you've lost something very dear to you."

She wanted to be angry at him for digging, but he spoke the truth. She did need reassurance, at least to be enlightened her life was worth living. What else could she do—wallow in self pity for the rest of her days?

"All those people are dead because I was selfish," she said, breaking down into a sob. "And now he's dead because of it. I just don't know what to do."

Ian went to her and sat down by her side. She immediately fell into his arms as he tried to comfort her with a soft hush.

"No, it's not your fault," he said in a soothing voice, stroking her hair with the palm of his hand. "Life has a funny way of making us believe we're to blame, but it really isn't our burden. Whatever happened, I'm sure it's fixable. You just have to have faith."

She sat up and looked him in the eye. He was desperately trying to make her feel better. And though it almost sounded as if he understood, he truly had no idea.

"I do understand," he said with a grin, and then sighed as he leaned back in the couch. "I lost my second wife about five years ago. She was driving too fast, coming home from a doctor's appointment to tell me we were finally going to have a baby, but a truck crossed the road in front of her. She didn't have time to brake."

"That's just heartbreaking," Katherine said somberly. "It must have been very hard to accept."

"I blamed myself for not going with her like I'd promised." He lowered his brows angrily. "Instead I stayed here, working on my damn music." He breathed a short, irritated breath through his nose. "It's all I have now. But I make the most of it, believing she would want me to continue."

"I'm sure she's proud."

He rested his eyes on her, curiously changing his gloomy appearance to a quizzical glance. She wondered what intriguing thought had just crossed his mind.

"About the song you heard in the car," he said. "You knew how it ended." He pulled his body forward, resting his elbows on his knees again. "I'm curious how you knew, when the words to my song aren't completely finished yet."

A tingling chill crawled over her skin. The way he looked at her, perplexed yet terribly intrigued to know her answer, but she didn't have one.

"I saw the entire thing this morning," he continued.

"Saw what?" she asked nervously, hoping he wasn't going to turn into some psychotic episode.

"I've gone to Stonehenge everyday waiting for some event to happen, but mostly I go to clear my mind. I find inspiration there. Then suddenly, I see a woman appear out of thin air right in front of me." He chuckled. "And now here you are, sitting in my living room. And I have no idea what to do except sit here and stare at you. For you remind me of someone I knew a long time ago—absolutely lovely just as she was."

Katherine quickly stood up, afraid of what strange ideas were lurking in his mind. She backed toward the front door, eager to escape out into the night.

"No," he stated, clearly realizing she was alarmed. "I didn't mean to scare you. I was only mentioning what an amazing thing it is to see. I just can't imagine what you've gone through to cause you so much pain."

She kept her eyes solid on him as he stood on his feet. He walked toward the kitchen, and then turned with a wave for her to follow.

"Come on. Let me pour you a drink."

She hesitated, unsure of his intentions. But she'd followed him this far already, so there was no point in backing out now.

"If I may offer you some information," he said as he poured water into a glass and held it out to her as she walked in. "Today is Friday, August fourth, two thousand, six. I just found out yesterday some up-and-coming band is going to buy my song—the one you heard on the plane a year ago. Now," he continued eyeing her carefully as she took the glass from his hand. "If you ask me, that's a tad out of the ordinary. So I imagine you've somehow found your way through time. Am I correct in assuming this?"

Katherine sat down in the kitchen chair, thoughts swirling through her flabbergasted mind. Derrick had sent her through the same rift, but somehow she'd found her way into the past—months earlier than when she left.

She glanced down at the orb she'd refused to let out of her grasp. A hint of silver began to show as if telling her something was definitely happening here.

"I can tell by the look on your face I'm correct, and you're not where you're supposed to be." He took a drink from his glass and grinned. "Imagine what someone could do with time travel."

Katherine's eyes lit up. All this time, she'd been suffering in anguish, when she should have taken the time to think about her situation. If she'd gone back into time, then he'd still be in his resting place at the bottom of the English Channel.

"Ian," she said, barely able to speak from anticipation. "Do you know anyone who owns a charter with a heavy crane?"

He looked surprised, maybe even a bit overwhelmed by her sudden enthusiasm, but he nodded. "My brother owns one. It's in

Hastings, but I'm sure he'll be happy to take you where you need to go."

The feeling was unbearable as hope streamed through her body at an unbelievable rate. Without thinking, she jumped into Ian's arms, celebrating over what could possibly be the chance to make things right.

Chapter Sixteen

Excitement rushed over Katherine like a cleansing, washing remnants of sorrow as they lowered his coffin carefully to the floor of the fishing boat. Wood creaked eerily as it was set down by the long arm of the crane.

This was it—the moment of truth, the moment she'd finally get him back. It'd been five days, but it had felt like an eternity. But as she looked over the large green box, her face suddenly fell flat.

"This isn't the same one," she said scanning it with her eyes, studying it carefully before she fully made up her mind. Remembering the indention from the last one she'd dealt with, she could tell for sure. "Yes," she continued with a nod. "There's definitely something different about this particular coffin."

Ian scratched his head in puzzlement. "If you and this man went through a rift at a later time, when these people had already buried him, I would assume there might be two boxes in the water. I mean, if he was buried a second time in the same manner."

"It would make sense if it was the same people, but it couldn't have been. This one is different than the other, so maybe this is the Derrick I left a few days ago," she muttered under her breath, teeming in excitement. For if this was true then he wouldn't be a stranger again.

"Well then, there's only one way to find out," Ian said, briefly eyeing his brother who'd stood beside him in awkward silence the entire time. He returned his attention on her. "So what do we do now?"

She sighed. She never thought of what she'd do when she got here, and a shrug just seemed so melancholy, especially when everything had led up to this one defining moment. How would she get the box to open this time?

"The orb," she said aloud. "This is why he gave it to me. It's the key to opening ..." Her voice immediately dropped as a shimmer of light caught the corner of her eye.

She raised her hand inspecting the orb as it beamed with a luminous ray of gold. And within its spectacular display came darkness as black as the gem itself. It was absolutely stunning, but she had no time to enjoy the vision.

As if her hand had a mind of its own, it immediately fell onto the coffin, placing the orb down firmly onto the lid. It skimmed across, pulling a completely mystified Katherine down the length of it until it suddenly stopped at the edge.

At first nothing happened, though everything fell eerily still, including the water underneath the ship. Birds that had sung non-stop since they arrived in the cove suddenly hushed, and a frightening sensation swept over her—dead silence.

The golden glow began to brighten around her hand, slowly making its way up her arms. Spectacular rays engulfed her body with warmth, a magic unrestrained and terribly arousing. And then her hand immediately sunk down inside the box as if it were nothing but a mold of liquid.

She could see nothing but light beyond the misty black rings. It felt marvelous caressing her skin, deeply penetrating her thoughts with love as she caught glimpse of Derrick's face within the light.

A sigh escaped her lips as she reached out, sharing the light with him when she touched his handsome face. There wasn't anything she could do to stop tears from forming in her eyes, for the sensation was heart-wrenching, yet terribly addicting as the light began to fade along with his glorious form, leaving her wanting more.

The top of the coffin slid perfectly to the side. It hit the floor of the ship with such force the wood cracked beneath its weight. Large splinters stabbed the air as it came to rest at the base of the coffin.

"I'm so sorry," she whispered, feeling a bit dizzy from what she gathered was her first experience with magic. "I'll pay for the damages."

"It is fine," Ian said in an odd, unenthused tone, for his sights were explicitly on what was inside the coffin. "Will he rise immediately? Or will it take time?" he asked aloud as if asking the wind in a whisper.

"I don't know," she replied, excitement looming inside her.

A moment of silence went by as she watched the water inside the coffin. She wished something would happen, anything, but there was nothing.

"It might take a little while," Ian said in a reassuring voice. "We could take this time to head back to—"

The water suddenly gurgled, startling all three of them into stepping back away from it, but Katherine immediately found her way to its side. Watching as the gurgle came to a rolling boil, she couldn't help but worry. Was this normal? Was this the way it happened when she released him the first time?

A human-like body took shape inside the coffin, but kept to a watery form as it slowly sat up in the still air. A warm blue mist caressed it as silky white streams swirled inside the figure, as if threading an existence, making him whole again.

Her heart sank when she saw him. Warm streams blanketed her face as his perfect form eerily stepped out of the watery grave to face her.

He was weak as he fell forward into her arms and took his first breath, no doubt the first in many thousands of years. A watery cough followed as if he'd drowned but was suddenly revived.

She shivered at the coldness of his skin, finding her pleading gaze on Ian's astounded face. And as if he'd read her mind, he quickly went off to retrieve a blanket.

As she held Derrick in her arms, she met the eyes of Ian's brother. The look on his face was blank, expressionless as he watched her, just how he'd been throughout the entire trip. He was strange, and his demeanor like a useless tree—careless and stiff.

"Thank you," she said, feeling terribly uncomfortable. A normal man would at least acknowledge her with a welcome, but he stood as still as ever without a word.

"I realize this is probably the most unbelievable thing you've ever seen," she said as she glanced down at Derrick, admiring the way his eyes were on her in the same loving manner she remembered. "It's the same for me."

The grin she presented Derrick felt surreal. At the moment, when Ian covered his naked body with the blanket, her heart grew warm. It'd been five days of being lost, but now he was finally here with her. It was where he belonged. And as she believed fate should have it, he'd be forever by her side.

"Katherine," Derrick whispered as he palmed her cheek with a weak hand. "You found me."

"Did you ever doubt?" she asked as she cradled his head in her hands, gazing down into his crystal green eyes.

"Ten-thousand years," he said as his body lit up into a flaming sea, anger curiously swallowed him with an intense glow. She wondered if he was angry with her, though she couldn't quite blame him. After all, this was her fault.

With her help, he found the strength to stand on his feet, pulling the blanket around him as he wearily turned to face Ian and his expressionless brother. In discontent, he glared at them.

"Ten-thousand years I have kept the memory inside me, willing myself never to forget the face that damned me to another lonely death."

Katherine wondered why he staggered toward Ian saying these disturbing things. Had he truly been imprisoned for that long? A punishment like this certainly would bring someone to immeasurable insanity.

She quickly stepped in front of him, blocking his clear path to Ian. "Everything will be fine now," she said as she put her arms around his waist, stopping him from his unstable walk. She pressed her face against his cool chest, dousing his angry aura. "I'll take care of you. We can live here now, and everything will be perfect."

"I'm sorry, Katherine," he said. His tone was softer, but the anger still held precedence. "There is much you need to know. Everything that happened after you left," he said, gritting his teeth in angry sorrow. "Our foolish desires must end here—now. It has to for the sake of both worlds."

She lifted her eyes to his, appalled by his hurtful words, but terribly intrigued by them. "What terrible things did they put you through?"

"Ask your guides," he said in a disgusted tone. "They deceive you."

"What are you talking about?" Ian asked, surprised by his words.

"He followed you through the rift, ordered by his master to watch you and wait for the opportune time to retrieve the diamond."

"It can't be," Katherine argued. "I was completely alone when I went through."

"There are certain destinations within each passage, but uncertain times. He must have arrived here long before you and had to wait."

"This is crazy," Ian said defensively, pleading Katherine with grave eyes. "I can't believe you're listening to this."

She didn't know what to believe. Ian was perfectly normal, as ordinary as any other man she'd met, though conveniently placed. But his brother, something was definitely off with him.

"How do you know you can trust your thoughts?"

Derrick sighed, lowering his brow. "I watched as he transformed, taking on life. His obedience to his master may be to fulfill his own desires, but he remains loyal. He is here only for the magic."

"If he only wants the gem, why didn't he take it when we met? Why would he help me find you?"

"You fail to remember, Katherine. Only the guardian can perform the ritual," Derrick said, lowering his eyes to hers. "You are pure magic, the daughter of Koran. The gem is the key to your power, and they wish to take it from you."

Katherine, completely dumbfounded, glanced down at the black gem in her palm. She hadn't a clue what this meant for her, nor did she really care. It was all words to her. And though she'd witnessed it first hand with Derrick's resurrection, it was the orb that had guided her.

If he believed there was something suspicious here, then she would believe as well. And as if opening her eyes for the first time, she watched Ian nervously shift his feet.

His face became twisted as he returned her glance. "I—" he stammered, realizing Derrick's words had convinced her. And then he sighed. "I truly am sorry, Katherine."

Ian's brother suddenly looked at him, glaring as if he were pressing his eyes into his skull. A look of utter hatred presented him with his first unstill moment.

"I never really wanted this," Ian continued, ignoring the defiant stare.

"You were the one at the temple," Derrick said as he shielded Katherine with his body.

"Yes," Ian replied. "And now by Katherine's journey to this time, history has changed. The universe didn't suffer darkness right away. But he now knows where the diamond is, and will stop at nothing to get it."

"Wait," she interrupted him, terribly lost in this conversation. "You were me in the temple?"

Ian nodded. "I didn't want to fool you, but I had to. I am his chosen—an Atlantean without permission to pass into the afterlife until I have guided enough souls across the river. It is punishment for the sins I committed against him."

"You're the ship bearer?" Derrick asked in complete awe.

"Yes," he replied with a sigh. "When he closed off the river, we were forced to attack the city and kill our own people, collecting their power for his purpose. But when the diamond left Atlantis, the river could not extend any farther."

"What happens now?" Derrick asked. "Will you obey his command and take her back to him? You should know I won't allow anything to happen to her," he added angrily.

"Unfortunately, he has almost enough power to open a single rift without it. Though he can't control the universe without the magic in the gem, he will bring his army through. And when this happens, the earth will become his river, and another gathering of souls will strengthen his rein to rule the universe."

In a bizarre change of mood, Ian grinned. He let out a short laugh through his nose, looking to Derrick as if he were an old buddy ready to head to the pub for drinks.

"I've been here for over two-hundred years stuck in this body he gave me, waiting for her to come through. I was supposed to only come a few days ahead and prepare for her sacrifice, as well as yours, but you know how rifts are." He chuckled lightly. "But as I waited, I found this world had a certain appeal, and began to love the idea of staying."

His smile slowly turned to frown, returning his attention to Katherine. "He constructed me to be a perfect human for this purpose—to gain your trust when we met, to blend in with the people to make my mission easier to perform. But I found love, which is something I have not done since ..." His voice trailed for a moment as he looked at Katherine. "So I decided when you finally came through the rift, I would help you instead."

Derrick sat down beside Katherine with a softened face. "You know the consequence of defying your master." He looked at Ian with sudden respect in his eyes. "He will never let you go."

Katherine stood up in frustration. "Just tell me who you're both talking about! Who is he?"

Her sudden outburst startled both men. The ship began to roll as the water was released from its silence. Birds began to chirp again as the air was restored around them.

Katherine felt a cool breeze on her warm skin, shaken a bit by the sudden release of sound. And though it was completely bizarre, she'd finally learned to put up with the abnormal and not question it.

"We're not leaving this cove until you answer me."

"I'm sorry," Ian said somberly. "But she needs to know the truth. You both do."

Derrick watched Ian closely, wanting to deny him his wish, but he also knew he was right. He bowed his head as he stood up, not wanting to look anyone in the eye, especially Katherine who couldn't take her pondering glance off him.

"I will tell you," he said. "But we must find a safe place. For the moment you realize who you truly are, the magic will burst inside you."

"She will need to discover the magic within her," Ian said as he glanced at the empty space beside him where his brother had stood just moments before. "And she will need to do it quickly, for he will soon learn I've betrayed him again. And then he will come after us all."

Chapter Seventeen

Paradise—a meeting of a clear blue sea and soft white sand underneath a cloudless sky was just how it was supposed to be in Bimini.

According to the photos Katherine found on the internet, she should be lying in a hammock between two palm trees, soaking comfortably in the heat of the sun. She should be sipping on a tropical drink from a coconut cup decorated with vibrant colored umbrellas while a warm breeze played in her hair. She should be relaxing.

But paradise wasn't what this trip was supposed to be about. If only it had held up its bargain of being perfectly serene, a retreat worthy of taking, this unworldly task would be a little easier to understand. Dark clouds refused her the glorious rays from the heavens and only offered dreariness worthy of the misery she was now in.

As she stood in the pouring rain listening as Derrick went on about controlling the flame she'd somehow conjured in her hand, tears formed in her eyes. Tiredness had set in a long while ago, but he'd only pushed her harder. They'd been at this for more than ten hours without a break, and she was only now beginning to realize a fragment of this extraordinary magic she supposedly carried.

She wished he'd go back to how he presented his first words. They'd been calm and encouraging. Like a professor at a university he'd lectured, brows stern, eyes only on the matter at hand. But now his impatience was evident, as if this torrential rain had dampened his mood, which was exceedingly possible, for it had definitely turned hers for the worse.

Through soaked strands of hair, she watched this strange fire oddly staying lit in the downpour. It had begun with a flicker, igniting from the depths of her soul. And with an emotional conjugation of sorrow, anger, and love beyond anything she'd ever experienced before, it grew into a roaring flame.

Now swirling around in her palm like a slow moving twister, it patiently waited for her to set it loose across the water, just what the first one she'd conjured was supposed to do before it sunk like a rock. She only hoped Derrick wouldn't lose his remaining patience and scold her again for not listening to his direction. One more harsh word and she knew she'd break down into an exhausted sob.

"Feel your emotions," Derrick yelled, his serious tone stabbing the angry air. "Let them boil inside you as you concentrate on where you want them to go." He pointed out over the raging sea. "There."

Katherine stretched her arm out in front of her, holding her blazing palm upright. She held her breath in hopes this time she'd succeed. And as if she were letting go of all the tension inside her, she exhaled and released the flame.

With her eyes open wide, she watched as it quickly flew out over the restless waves, bringing her a smile she hadn't found since they began training. And when it flew up into the air and disappeared into the clouds, Derrick finally cracked a grin.

"Very good," he said with a nod. "Now see if you can do it again."

As tired as she was, her success brought her an instant second wind. Confidence brought forth an immediate flame, one much brighter than the other. And as she held it up before her, she could feel a little more control.

Concentrating on the flame, she breathed in deep through her nose. "I can sense it now," she said as she exhaled and let it go. It skimmed the waves, creating a parting of water with its speed. It lifted up into the sky, but this time created a gaping hole in the clouds.

Sunlight beamed magnificently on the water, casting a blue reflection. A rainbow appeared in the rays, but only for a short moment as the clouds began to gather again.

"Beautiful," Derrick whispered, smiling abundantly. But he wasn't looking out over the ocean.

Katherine turned to find him staring at her, eyes lit up magnificently. It took her a moment, but she finally realized it wasn't his eyes glowing, but a reflection of her own aura.

"It's beautiful," he said, palming her wet cheek. "If only you could see it. You bear the color of diamonds in phenomenal sunlight, for you have finally found the magic within you. Katherine," he continued as he pulled her into his arms, "you are the most beautiful thing I've ever seen. You are light. You are magic."

The thought, at first, made her feel warm, comfortable despite the cold rain. But as she thought, fear began to overtake her. This was an emotion she cared nothing for, but couldn't help but be overwhelmed by it.

"What's wrong?" he asked as he took her by the hand.

Afraid of what he might think, she pulled a quick white lie off the top of her head. "I don't want anyone to see me like this. People wouldn't understand." Not quite a lie, but enough to keep him from suspecting her fear.

"Only I can see your aura."

He chuckled nervously as he tucked her arm under his and led her up the beach toward the house Ian had bought years ago, just for this purpose. It was as if he'd planned all along to take care of her, as he'd decorated it in a woman's favor.

Or maybe he'd brought his wife here, and this place was her legacy. Sweet sorrow thought Katherine as she made her way up the beach ramp and stepped inside the foyer.

She immediately pulled off her wet clothes and went to the bedroom closet. She had to admit, Ian's wife certainly had taste. Not one garment was shabby enough to wear for lounging, which was a bit unfortunate. She'd give anything for a pair of sweats and a T-shirt, but instead she pulled out a lovely black sundress.

"You look worn," Derrick said as he watched her from the doorway.

"Maybe a little," she replied, a bit startled by his presence for she hadn't realized he'd been watching her.

He came to stand before her and lifted his hand to her face. With an eager glance, he stroked her cheek with the back of his hand.

"I'm sorry," he whispered, eyeing her intently. "I pushed you too hard today."

"I'm fine," she said, smiling graciously, enjoying his tender attention, for he'd been with her for weeks, but never offered a gentle touch until now.

"Your eyes tell me differently," he continued. "But you have to know why I push you."

For a moment he stood staring into her eyes. She yearned for his touch, to feel his lips on hers. To feel his arms around her, caressing, massaging would arouse a desire for him to take her to bed. She closed her eyes, hoping he'd take her there, but his hand slipped away from her face.

"Ian must have come here recently and prepared for our arrival," he said, clearing his throat nervously. He arched his brow in a curious manner as he stopped in the doorway and glanced back.

She wanted to be frustrated with him. If he didn't look so good, standing in the doorway, wearing nothing but his pair of black slacks, still wet from the day ... And she stood in her undergarments, most likely looking like a drowned rat. It was no wonder he moved away.

But she closed the distance, finding herself standing before him in the doorway, unable to keep from touching his bare chest. "It's been so long since you've put your arms around me."

She pressed her body against him, gently pulling at his skin with her lips. She wanted him in a desperate way, and she could tell by the way he breathed, he wanted her as well, but he moved away.

"What's wrong?" she asked, trying to catch her breath, so as not to cry.

"We don't have time for this," he said, searching the nearby table for something. He found the tie he used to pull his black locks away from his face and proceeded to do it without another glance.

"You've forgotten about the night we shared in the temple," she said, swallowing down her tears.

"I could never forget," he sternly replied. "I know you want answers. I swear I'll give them to you when you complete your training. And then I will hold you as often as you like."

"You've changed," she said disappointedly. "Have you fallen out of love with me?"

"I will never deny my feelings for you," he replied. "It is difficult to resist you while you stand there in your bare skin. But we cannot let our guard down, not even for a moment."

"Everything feels so strange to me. It's like this magic comes from somewhere else, but not from me."

She walked away from his puzzled glance. Anger, frustration, and confusion rolled through every vein in her body as she pulled a towel from the linen closet and draped it over the bar near the walk-in shower.

A man in love would never have turned her away just like he had. He would have become aroused and leapt at the chance to be with her intimately. It hurt.

She knew answers would come eventually, though he'd been promising to tell her everything since they met. But as she stepped in the shower, she wondered if there even was a truth to be told.

Warmth had finally returned to her skin as she toweled off and slipped on the dress. Though her hair was still damp, she tied it back and stepped into the bedroom.

"She's not ready," Derrick said with a sigh, speaking to someone over the phone. "It took much too long for her to tap into the power. Something must be wrong."

"What do you think it is?" she heard Ian ask.

"I don't know."

"If you truly love her, you'll sacrifice everything. She needs you now, more than you know. And you will need her."

Katherine listened to the silence, hoping to hear Derrick's confession. But he never said a word, only clearing his throat as if the very thought of it was ridiculous.

"If truths are not discovered, it won't be long until he is able to come through. This world will surely die." Ian's voice became distraught. "You understand what you need to do."

"I don't." Derrick gave a frustrated sigh.

Katherine quickly made her way to the door, expecting answers. Ian obviously had more faith in her than he did. And she knew she could handle it, no matter what this big secret was.

"Hades will rule everything. Death will be certain as hell is brought to the surface."

"Hades?" Katherine whispered, puzzled at the mention of his name.

"If she can't handle the power, I'll extract it and do it myself."

That was enough eavesdropping for her. And as she walked out into the room, Derrick hung up the phone.

"How was your shower?" he asked quickly as if nothing was wrong.

"Is all of this really about Hades?" she asked.

"What are you talking about?"

"Don't patronize me," she yelled. "I heard everything you and Ian said over the phone."

"It is not wise for you to speak his name," he said, finding strength in his voice.

"Why not?"

"If you say his name when you realize who you are..."

"Hades!" she shouted, interrupting him. "Hades, Hades, Hades!"

He quickly grabbed her before she could say it anymore. Covering her mouth with his hand, he twisted her around, holding her tight against him. With clenched teeth, he pressed his lips to her ear.

"You are not ready," he growled angrily.

Tears formed in her eyes. It was true then. Hades destroyed the Atlanteans, and was threatening to destroy everything on Earth— but how could it possibly be?

Unable to breathe, she struggled to free herself. He let go of her mouth, but kept her hard against him.

"It's not true," she said in a gasping breath. "It can't be."

"Believe it," he demanded hatefully.

"Why should I?" she asked, cringing from his hurtful grasp on her arms.

Derrick sighed and loosened his grasp. He slid his hands down to hers and held them, squeezed them, and then again pressed his lips to her ear.

"I will tell you," he strained his voice in a whisper and then let out a long sigh. "The gem in your hand holds Hades' black heart. He wants it back, for it also holds Koran's power. It was given to you because you are their daughter."

She shook her head. "No," she whispered, controlling her trembling voice. "I'd feel different if it were true, wouldn't I?"

He tightened his grip on her hands. "Only when you say his name."

"I'll say it and prove it's not true."

"Don't be foolish," he growled again. "You're not ready."

Without releasing his grasp on her hands, he enveloped her in his arms. Like being stuck in a straight jacket, she found she couldn't move. And no matter how much she struggled, he only held tighter.

"I'm just an ordinary woman stuck in a terrible nightmare," she whispered, closing her eyes. She breathed in deep, and held it for a moment, hoping she was making the right decision. And when she exhaled, she blurted out his name.

"Hades."

Derrick held on to her, ready to shield the explosion of power that was supposed to burst from her. She knew in her heart nothing would happen, and for a moment, everything remained silent. But her palm suddenly began to tingle, and a pulse of black mist quietly began to creep from the gem.

With her hands still in his, she turned to face him, finding anger and curiousness mingling in his eyes. Uncertainty emitted from hers and she now wondered if she'd been too hasty in her decision.

Like a breath of air, dark essence encircled them. It caressed them as they stood face to face, wondering and worrying what was about to happen. And with her hands bound tightly to his, she feared the worst.

"I'm sorry," she whispered as she met his tentative eyes, knowing her apology was worthless to the destruction she'd leave behind once this horrible power was unleashed. And as if this were her last moment of life, she rose to meet him in a kiss.

His lips were soft. As she brushed hers against them, all her emotions began to surface—sorrow, remorse, and love, just how she'd felt when she released her magic across the waves.

Tears formed in her eyes as she let go of his hands and slid her arms around his neck. And as he finally welcomed her embrace, passionately, enticingly, and sorrowfully returning the kiss, she let her emotions go.

The earth rumbled beneath their feet, making the floor roll like ocean waves, forcefully separating them from their ardent moment. The house began to shake violently causing the hangings on the walls to fall to the floor. Glass shattered, lights flickered, and then suddenly all went eerily quiet.

Darkness hid the late afternoon, leaving them in a state of shadow. Katherine found her way back into Derrick's arms and led him to the bedroom doorway, swallowing down fears she despised.

In a surreal instant, the gem loosened from her skin and fell to the floor. The sound seemed loud in her ears, as if someone had dropped a brick from the roof of a two-story building. She watched as the gem rolled across the living room floor until it oddly came to rest at the front door, as if somehow it was summoned there.

Helicopters began to fly over the house flashing search lights in the dark sky, and skimming the waters below as if whatever they were looking for was right in front of them.

Curious, Katherine walked to the front door and picked up the gem. She made her way out to the front porch and stood in absolute wonder at the sight before her.

A road built of stone had risen from the ocean stretching from the beach to beyond the horizon. Under black storm clouds, the stones looked dark as night, and certainly appeared unworldly, especially to the gathering people on the beach.

"The road to Atlantis," Derrick said as he stepped out beside her. He grabbed the wooden banister and leaned his head between his arms. "I don't know what to do now," he whispered through clenched teeth.

She slid her hand over his shoulder. "I'll find a way to fix this," she said, hoping her words would comfort him, but she too, suffered the same bleak outlook.

People gathered on the beach near the road. Some even found their way onto it, with certain trepidation.

"We had more time," Derrick said with a look of defeat. "But now he'll come for us, and the universe will succumb to his darkness. Everything will be lost."

An icy chill swept over her. She felt it could lift her off her feet and take her out to sea just as her eyes turned that way. She'd made a detrimental mistake of not trusting Derrick's word, and now she would be the one person who caused the earth's destruction, and the immortal beings would be trapped in an eternity of torment.

Through blurred vision, she watched as the ocean waters began to bleed a dark substance, like oil seeping its way slowly toward the beach. Boats were consumed, and the people making their way onto the stones were devoured by it.

The others lining the beach began to scream, running in fear toward the street as dark figures fell from the sky like ghosts coming to haunt the shore. They landed on the newly risen road humming a malevolent song as they crept up to the beach. But they abruptly stopped at the dark waters edge, and the hum faded out like an ending to a sad song.

"Why did they stop?" Katherine whispered as she watched them in the eerie silence.

Derrick pulled from her tight clutch and cautiously made his way down the steps. When his feet touched the sand, he turned around and tossed her a compelling glance. His turquoise glow radiated beautifully, causing her heart to break as if she knew this was his way of saying goodbye, and there was nothing she could do to stop him.

Tears fell from her eyes as he walked to the shore and stopped within an arms length of the souls. Careful not to touch them, he stood and waited.

If she could take a picture now, she'd win a Pulitzer. She'd show the world this remarkable image of man meeting unworldly darkness as it slowly extended from the black clouds in the sky. A skull enveloped in black haze rained downward, and stopped just above the army as it exhaled a frigid wind across the beach.

Katherine shivered, clutching the gem tighter in her hand. She would do whatever she could to keep it away from this thing, even if it meant sacrificing herself.

"Let them go," Derrick shouted without fear, causing the eerie song to begin again.

In a deep breathy voice, the skull demanded his dark army to hush, and the hum immediately faded.

As Katherine watched, her hand began to tingle, just like it had done before. She nervously brought it to her eyes, feeling a strange pulse, as if it were somehow trying to communicate. Unsure of what she was supposed to do, she breathed a heavy sigh.

Deep in her frightful mind, a voice spoke her name. Soothing to her ears, it was beautiful and forgiving, like an angel from heaven. And in a bizarre moment, everything around her came to a halt.

"Who are you?" Katherine asked.

An image appeared before her, a woman, glowing radiantly with a familiar sea-green blush. Her smile beamed heavenly and her white flowing gown feathered around her feet as she walked toward her through the still air.

Katherine could tell by her slightly bowed head she had no ill intentions. And when she drew close enough, she could see a rounded mark on her forehead, empty and dark beneath long golden hair.

"I know who you are ..." Katherine's voice trailed as she swallowed down anxious revelation. "You're Koran, my mother."

The woman raised her bright eyes to hers, but she solemnly shook her head. "I am indeed Koran, but I am not your mother," she said in a soft voice, one a true mother might use to calm her child's cries. "You have been deceived by so many, it is no wonder you are confused."

Koran's eyes turned solemn as she looked at her lovingly. Her eyes radiated as she gently touched her arm, soothing her broken heart and her cluttered mind.

"There are many things to discuss," she continued. "But we have not time to dwell on mistakes and unanswered questions. It is time to end this darkness and save this world."

Katherine stood up and wiped her cheeks with the back of her hand. "But I can't," she pleaded. "I don't have the power to do this."

"It is not your burden." Koran reached out and took her by the hand. She gently opened it to reveal the gem, glowing magnificently, but strangely it was no longer black. White light radiated from it, and suddenly Katherine's aura lit up, just as it had done before.

"My son's heart is pure now." Koran eyed Derrick as he stood near the darkness, unknowingly waiting for the release of time. "I poured my magic into him when he was born, in hopes it would purify the darkness within him, but it did not work, for mine was tainted as well," she said as she returned her attention to Katherine's astonished glance. "I had no choice but to extract his heart and bury it inside the gem, for it was the only way to keep him safe. For years I hid it from the eyes above, tucked away in the stone crevice of the temple. But my own child found it as if somehow he had been drawn to its power, just as his father was lured by its darkness."

"Then how did I get it?"

Koran gave a sorrowful sigh. "The pure magic I gathered in the heavens went into a newborn child so she could hold the darkness of the gem, a bind, if you will. She was sent into this world so our eyes would be hidden from its existence. You are that child,

Katherine, daughter of Ian and Ezra."

Katherine covered her mouth with her free hand, eyes wide with distraught—speechless. She leaned back against the banister feeling faint as she turned her questioning eyes to the dark image on the beach.

Had Derrick kept this from her all this time? Was he so secretive that he kept his true identity from her as well? But as her eyes wandered over his dark facade, she knew in her heart he was lied to as well. As he stood ready to face his unrealized father bravely, ready to die to save her and her world, she loved him more than ever.

A sudden spark of anger caught her eyes. "You took me away from my family for what purpose?"

"I can answer that." A familiar voice came from behind her. She turned to find Ian standing in the doorway with sympathetic eyes. He joined them on the deck, completely fascinated by the image on the beach. Shaking his head in astounded silence, he folded his arms over his chest.

"It never ceases to amaze me when time stands still," he said, briefly eyeing Koran. "It's hard to believe it until you've witnessed it first hand."

The grin he wore was not from the thrill of the moment, but was rightly from apprehension. But when he turned his attention to Katherine, his eyes suddenly lit up with pride.

"I've wanted to tell you so many times, but I was not allowed." He gently thumbed a tear falling down her cheek. "It was an honor to us that Koran chose you. You saved her child from certain death."

"But the choice you made caused many others to die."

"I know my mistakes," Koran said. "I hoped the gem would never return, but it did, and now he will stop at nothing to get it back. And if he attains all that power..."

"Everything will fall at his feet," Katherine whispered the rest of her sentence, dismay written in her wary eyes. "What do I do?"

A moment of silence went by as both Koran and Ian somberly looked at each other. She became worried.

"Just tell me what I'm supposed to do," she demanded.

Ian pulled Katherine around to face him, squeezing her arms gently with his loving hands. He breathed a somber breath and bowed his head. He took her by the hand and opened it to reveal the gem.

"This is not only his heart you carry in your hand, but it is now yours as well. They became one when you made love to him in the sacred temple, which was not foreseen to happen."

She slightly blushed at his knowledge of their rendezvous. "I didn't realize."

"Unfortunately, the path you took led you here, and now you must destroy the gem. This is what all your trials have led to, and is the path you must now take."

Katherine reflexively grasped the gem tight, outraged by such a request. And by the look in Ian's eyes, and the way Koran refused to look at her, she knew the outcome of completing such a task.

She shook her head. "Why can't I just keep it with me, and hide it again?"

"No being can hide from love, dear child," he replied earnestly.

"Derrick will die if I destroy it. Won't he?" she asked as tears flowed from her eyes.

"A soul cannot survive without the heart, not even the immortals. But it will not be his death alone. Koran will join his fate. And ..." His voice trailed. And it was then she realized what he meant—her heart was also entangled in the gem.

"I'll die too," she whispered.

A moment of silence went by, but it felt like an eternity. Katherine's thoughts ran rampant, trying to think of another way to stop this from happening. To destroy four hearts, including her own, was nothing short of a nightmare—and it was her responsibility to bring it to an end.

There was no where to run this time. Atlantis was destroyed. And he'd found his way into this world, giving her no other option but to do as they asked. She had to destroy the gem.

"Then tell me how," she said, feeling the desperation to put this to an end.

"Go to him," Ian replied. "Place the gem on the road and strike it hard with a stone. It is the only way."

"You must hurry," Koran added stressing her concern. "I cannot hold time much longer."

"I wish I would have found you sooner," she said, palming Ian's face, and without another thought, she quickly pulled away.

She ran down the steps and sprinted frantically through the

sand, making her way toward the still black sea. The clouds around Hades' skull began to billow, but ever so slowly. There was still time to awake Derrick from time, and solemnly say her goodbye.

In tears, she grabbed his hand and pulled him into her arms. The glow of the gem surrounded them with a light so immense that all darkness faded. He awoke from his paused slumber and gazed at her with loving eyes.

"Are you all right?" he asked briefly glancing around. But his eyes returned to hers, causing her to melt into his arms yet again.

"I love you, Derrick. I wish I had time to tell you everything before ..."

He gently pulled her chin up with a curled finger, forcing her to look at him. With a sweet grin, he swiped a lock of her dark hair from her tear-filled eye.

"I am glad to hear you speak such beautiful words from your sweet lips, but there is no reason to fret our situation."

"You don't understand," she said as her lips began to tremble. "Everything you've ever known is a lie ..."

"Enough," he interrupted as he squeezed her arms gently in his hands.

"But I need to tell you the truth."

"And I need you to listen to me now," he stressed in seriousness, for their brief moment in time was beginning to fade. "When time resumes, I'll distract him long enough for you to slip through the rift behind him. I don't know where you'll end up, but at least you'll be safe for a little while."

"No," she said, shaking her head. "I won't leave you again! This time you're coming with me." Her heart stung fiercely, remembering the last time they were separated.

"You have to do this, Katherine."

"I can't leave without you," she strongly urged, holding tight to his shirt. "I won't."

He quickly pulled her close. "Trust in me," he whispered in her ear. "Let your heart guide you."

"But my heart is with yours," she cried.

He leaned down and kissed her softly, but it grew into an urgent longing as she wished for more time. She slid her arms around his neck, holding him, afraid to let go as he caressed her, but he gently pushed her away.

"I love you, Katherine," he said as he slowly backed away from her. "No matter what happens, I will always be thinking of you."

Darkness eerily settled over them as the skull finally caught up with the moment. It wasted no time in finding Derrick. And with an open mouth, it drifted his way, emitting a frigid breath as it prepared to consume him, but he faced it with a confident stance.

"Go now!" he shouted to her, pointing at the stone behind the skull, but she couldn't do as he asked—not this time.

There were so many instances where she'd listened to his advice and had followed without question, but only to come out with more unanswered questions. No, this time would be different. This time, she would not run away.

She made her way to his side, ready to face this terrible burden together. She wouldn't let him die for her again—never again. And though she knew he was furious with her decision, she wasn't about to give in to what he wanted.

"Leave now, Katherine!" he yelled, pushing her slightly toward the road, but she wouldn't mind him.

"I won't end our lives by destroying the gem," she said, assertively eyeing Ian who still stood on the deck watching in awe. "And I will not run away ever again."

In total confidence, she quickly summoned the fire she'd worked on the entire day. With a steady hold on it, she glared at the skull as it began to descend toward her. She was ready for him—ready to exhale her power and put a hole in this terrible dark essence invading her world.

"Katherine," Derrick said as he picked her up in his arms, immediately dousing the controlled fire in her palm.

"What are you doing?" she screamed. "Put me down so I can do this!"

He carried her to the water's edge, ignoring the dark souls reaching for them with their black fingers. He leapt up onto the road beside the rippling wave of the rift and set her down on her feet. With a quick twist, he turned her around to face it.

"I'm not going," she cried, holding herself back as he tried to push her in.

She reached behind her and grasped his shirt. With all her might, she held on as tight as she could, and somehow found the strength to turn around and face him. But just as she did, her eyes widened in horror, and the enormous black skull opened its misty jaws and swallowed them both.

Chapter Eighteen

Glorious light surrounded Katherine in her dark abyss. Floating in a boat on calm waters hazily brought her to an awakened state. The light faded.

He'd consumed them. The last image of his descent still lingered fresh in her mind. She had closed her eyes and held on to the man she loved during their moment of imminent demise. Though now, as she floated along, it puzzled her.

A death from being swallowed by some dark entity should have certainly brought some sort of misery, but she hadn't felt a thing.

"Derrick!" She suddenly rose to her feet and scanned the small boat until she found him lying down in the floor at the other end.

With a careful step, she made her way to his side and knelt down on her knees. She hesitantly touched him, and found his skin cold. But his chest rose and fell, reassuring her thoughts he wasn't dead.

She lay down beside him and huddled close, offering her body for warmth, though she wasn't much warmer than he was. But it was all she could do to wait as the boat continued to drift, rocking slightly over a black sea, until he woke up.

Derrick finally stirred, and his movement caused Katherine to open her eyes. She lifted her body from his and met his confused stare with a relieving smile.

"You're finally awake," she said as she helped him sit up.

He held his aching head. "What happened?"

"I'm not sure," she replied with tears in her eyes. "But whatever it is, I know it's my fault."

He enveloped her in his arms, comforting her cries as he glanced around at their surroundings. The boat—its stained black wood was all too familiar. And the endless black sea was a sight he'd never wanted to see again, for it had held his immortal presence for thousands of years, dreadfully alone—limbo.

He groaned. "We'll be okay," he said as he pulled her up to him. With hands cupping her face, he kissed her lightly on the temple.

"I'm so cold," she whispered, and shivered when he pulled her against him.

His arms felt good around her, holding on to her tightly, comfortably. But he too was as cold as ice, and it made her thoughts wander in a direction she didn't want them to go.

"Are we dead?" she asked in a whisper, dreading his hesitation to answer her.

He sighed as he leaned his chin on her forehead, carefully searching for words. "Yes, Katherine, we are dead, but we haven't crossed the river yet."

She rose from his arms and keenly looked into his eyes. "Do you mean we're on the river—the river of death?"

He nodded, tossing her a solemn grin, but he didn't say a word. He just pulled her back into his arms and held her as close as he could.

"At least we are together," he said when he heard her softly cry. His heart ached for her, but he too was completely helpless to this void. "I have drifted here alone for many years waiting for someone to find me." He gently kissed her temple. "You were my savior once. I am sure of it."

She pressed her cheek against his chest. When she felt they were as close as two bodies could be, she closed her eyes.

"Our tragic end is not in vain," he continued with a whisper in her ear. "For as we sail across Styx, we will be together in an eternal embrace."

♦

She wasn't sure how long they'd been drifting, when she opened her eyes from sleep. Minutes, hours, maybe even days had passed. It was still terribly surreal, and the only thing keeping her from breaking down was the feeling of his arms around her.

He still slept as she slipped away from his cold embrace, but only to sit up and look around. She breathed in deep and then exhaled as she looked toward the night sky.

Finding the stars looked just as they did in Atlantis, she wondered if they'd been there before, emanating their beautiful pastel glow.

She couldn't remember, but it still made her smile, for it was nice to see something other than complete darkness surrounding them.

Finding a sudden eagerness to explore, she made her way to the edge of the boat and leaned over. She studied the black water wondering what would happen if she touched it. And curiously, she reached down.

She was hesitant, but finally found the calm water with her fingers, skimming them lightly over its thick substance. It was oddly warm when the air around her was as cool as a crisp fall morning.

She brought her fingers forward to her eyes, inspecting it curiously, but caught sight of something else below her. Just beneath her hand, down in the depths of the water, something moved. She eyed it cautiously as it swam to the surface and swirled around where she'd just touched. And as she sat up in the boat, it slowly lifted itself from the water.

She watched with wide eyes as it came to hover over her, ominous and black, oozing as if made of thick running water. Eyes of pearl it stared, eagerly awaiting acknowledgment, sending chills over her trembling body. And then it rolled out grim skeletal fingers, extending them to her as if it wanted her to take its hand.

Fear overwhelmed her as she backed away, shaking her head in disbelief. All this time they'd experienced quiet solitude, but here out of the dark waters was some unknown entity asking for her attention.

"The heart," it said in a profound breathy manner, emphasizing with a gesture for her to give it to him.

The faint memory of a black diamond came to her, but she shook her head, denying its existence. "I don't have it anymore."

With a horrifying growl, the dark being lunged for her, catching her by the throat. Its skeletal fingers grotesquely oozed black substance onto her skin.

She kicked the air with her bare feet as it lifted her out of the boat, rigid fingers tightening around her neck, strangling her. She struggled for breath, trying desperately to alert Derrick with a scream, and finally found her strained voice when she was suddenly dropped back inside the boat.

Gasping for her breath and fearing what might have happened if he hadn't saved her she stared at Derrick. He stood at the edge, looking over into the water as the substance quickly swam away from him as if somehow it was afraid. And then he turned just in time to catch her in his arms.

"Get us out of this place!" She breathed hard, desperately holding onto him.

"I'm sorry," he apologized, holding her tight as he sat them both back down in the floor of the boat. "I should have warned you about them."

"What are they?"

"They are murderers and thieves, criminals refusing to pass. Neither heaven nor hell wants them, so they stay in the river and make a nuisance of themselves."

She trembled uncontrollably. "How did he know?" she asked as she wiped tears from her eyes.

He pulled from her embrace with a curious glance. "Did he know something about you he should not?"

"He knew about the diamond," she replied in puzzlement. "I can't even remember much about it. So how does he?"

"Do you still have it?" he asked excitedly.

She shook her head. "I must have let it go when we were swallowed."

"Search the boat!" he demanded as he went to his hands and knees and began searching the floor.

"I don't understand," she said, curiously watching him, but finding this terribly familiar.

"If the dark souls are asking you for it, then he doesn't have it!"

It was instant as the entire memory of the gem came flooding back, like a tidal wave rushing over her, cleansing the darkness from her eyes. Touching the small pocket on the front of her dress, she sighed in relief. It was there, and a grin painted her face with excitement.

She reached into her pocket and fumbled it until it rested perfectly on her palm. She pulled it out and held it before her eyes, staring at its white glow seemingly growing brighter when Derrick caught sight of it.

She sat down and carefully held it up to him, knowing now what she'd meant to say before this all happened. "I remember trying to tell you the truth, but we were interrupted. And now," she said in a straight, cool voice. "You need to know who you are."

He looked at her with patience, and she knew this time she had his complete attention. There would be no more disruptions and no more chaotic instances to keep her from this moment. And as she handed him the gem, she could sense his confusion.

"It doesn't belong to me," she said as she dropped it on his palm. "It belongs to the true child of Koran, and that is you, Derrick."

He drew back with lowered brows. "Why are you saying this?"

"Koran came to me when you were with him on the beach. She stopped time to tell me everything."

"It's not true," he said trying to give her back the gem, but she refused.

"It is true." She raised her voice, terribly frustrated he wouldn't believe her. "Just accept it so we can leave. I want to go home."

"Take it back now!" he demanded, ignoring her plea.

"Doesn't it make sense?" she asked in a solemn breath massaging his rugged, unshaven face. "You clearly heard me say his name and nothing happened."

"You revived the road," he stubbornly growled.

"No," she said with a sigh. "I don't think I did—at least not alone. If you remember, you were holding my hand. Maybe you tried so hard to believe for me, it somehow reached the gem as if you were the one saying his name. Our hearts are intertwined inside."

"If what you say is true, then what now?" he asked. "What am I supposed to do with it?"

Katherine frowned slightly. It was so strange he'd known exactly what she had to do at the time, but now that the tables had turned, he hadn't a clue.

"Say his name," she said as she brought his hand up to her lips. She kissed his knuckles and then pressed his palm against her cheek. "I know you will believe …"

Her voice cut off when the boat suddenly jolted and rocked, as if something rather large hit it. Derrick quickly pulled her to the floor and huddled her beneath his protective arms.

"What was that?" she asked frantically.

"I'm not sure."

Another jolt rocked the boat, and an eerie hum came from the water. Katherine's eyes grew wide with fear, immediately recognizing the sound. It was happening again.

Dark substance rose from the water as if a thousand souls

suddenly united. They hovered over the boat, ready to release their black wave over them, but remained still in the air as if waiting for someone, or some thing to give the word.

Katherine huddled against Derrick. Afraid she'd be washed away, she held him tight, terrified they'd be separated and she'd spend an eternity alone on this forsaken river.

He pulled his hand up in front of her eyes and opened it to reveal the gem, still emanating radiant white. And when he looked at her once more, he cast a grin and closed it tightly in his hand.

"Koran!"

Katherine's light intertwined with his brilliant green sea. Their rich light gloriously drove the shadows back, purifying the water and turning the endless night into a spectacular blue sky.

The sun shone down, warming her skin for the first time in days. She bathed in it, turning around in heavenly rays, and then laughed as Derrick lifted her off her feet and swung her around in his arms.

"It's over," she said, pressing her temple to his and stealing a kiss from his lips. "That was easy."

Her words were spoken in earnest. But just after she said it, she didn't like how it made her feel. And by the look he was giving her, she could tell he felt the same.

She didn't want to ruin their moment. And the wondrous scenery gifting her eyes was enlightening and bright. But when he released her from his arms, the ending to their light was inevitable.

Dark water began to bleed from the horizon, creating a large wall of night. It careened toward them like a fast moving wave.

"No," Katherine whispered. "I don't want to go through this again."

"Have faith."

His voice brought her eyes back to his. Sorrow left his stare as the white light suddenly encircled them, creating a barrier of protection as the wave of souls splashed over them.

Katherine held tight, leaving her gaze on Derrick as he effortlessly held the light around them. A sudden flash of light came from the gem, blinding them both. And they stood together holding hands with eyes closed until the light began to fade.

It took a moment for her eyes to adjust, but Katherine was finally able to see where they were. With blue sky above her, waves rushing onto the sand, and the cries of seagulls in her ears, she knew this time this was real.

They stood on the beach in the same spot where they'd been swallowed, gazing over the stone road. And as if it beckoned them to walk its path, they climbed up on it.

"He has fled from your world now," Derrick said. "But now I must face him in mine."

Katherine nodded. "And I'm right behind you."

"No," he said as he gently grasped her hands in his. He lifted them to his lips and kissed them lightly. "Our journey together must end here."

"I was born in Atlantis. So I belong there … I belong there with you."

"My dear Katherine," he said as he pulled her into his arms and gazed into her eyes with such sweetness, a new love he carried for her. At that moment she saw his light, drowning the darkness he'd carried with him for so long. And when he lowered his mouth to hers in a kiss, her heart stung.

When they parted, his appearance had changed. No longer did he wear ragged clothes, but wore a radiant white shirt and slacks. His hair was clean and tied back away from his shaved face, making his beautiful turquoise eyes stand out. And she couldn't deny he was the most handsome man she'd ever laid eyes on, and the man she loved more than anyone.

Completely lost to his irresistible charm, she touched his face. "We've been through too much for me to lose you again." She cried pleading tears. "My heart can't take it."

"Katherine," he said as he gently lifted her hand, and with light in his eyes placed the gem on her palm. "This is yours now. It always has been."

"But you need it."

She urged to give it back, but he shook his head. "I don't need it anymore, for her light is inside me now," he said with a grin. "But I left my heart for you."

She grasped the gem tightly in her palm desperately crying as he lovingly wrapped his arms around her. Pressing her cheek to his chest, she broke down into an uncontrollable sob.

"I can't let you go," she said as she closed her eyes. "I love you too much."

He breathed a solemn sigh. "And I love you … more than words, but we must now say goodbye."

The sound of his heart thumped in her ear, matching the beat of hers. They were perfect together, no doubt in her mind—they belonged together. And no matter how far apart their bodies would be their souls would forever be intertwined in the stars.

She shut her eyes and held him tight, not knowing what to do now. She only wanted to stay in his arms and feel his gentle fingers caressing her skin, but somehow she knew he'd left her, for her arms had become hopelessly cold and empty.

Chapter Nineteen

Derrick walked the empty, desecrated streets of his city. A depressing and overwhelming sensation walked with him as he stepped through black water to get to the pyramid, for only there would he be able to perform his final task of severing the rifts.

A god of destruction would never be allowed to live in Atlantis, and would in no way be welcome in heaven. His immortal soul would be sacrificed to restore the magic in the land, and his body would finally give out in a true death.

He was ready for it. After thousands of years agonizing in darkness, he'd welcome this fate, but only after he made things right. And as he approached the top of the pyramid, the light around him began to burn bright.

His body suddenly lit up with white fire as he concentrated all his efforts on a vision, but no images came to mind. With all this terrible power inside him, something of the future should come, but it didn't.

He looked out at the destroyed structures below, his beloved city in ruins. And as he listened to the eerie hum of dark souls approaching, a horrifying thought crossed his mind. Maybe the darkness was inevitable, and Atlantis, along with its inhabitants, could never be resurrected.

He closed his eyes and began to chant the words he'd been taught to say, the fateful words to release Koran's magic from his body and heal his world. It hurt as the dark souls touched him, desperately trying to stop him, but he wouldn't give in to the pain.

He watched as the rips in the universe filled in, and his chance to leave this dark place was gone. His fate was sealed inside, and now he'd never see his beloved Katherine again.

The ground began to shake violently as he ascended into the

air. Light billowed off his being, an aura of unbound magic, as he chanted faster and with more control. The dark souls fled from him, making their way out over the city beginning to crumble from the fierce quake. And an enormous hole of darkness opened at the foot of the pyramid.

The buildings began to spiral around him, saturating the air with glittering gold and white sandstone. Ships began to break apart as wooden planks and floor boards ripped away. And their large masts bent and broke as their sails shredded like paper.

The earth tore up into pieces, sending trees and rocks through the air. And eventually everything in his world spun around him in one colossal whirlwind.

Instead of healing his world, he'd created devastation, an ultimate display of power not even darkness could control. Only one man, one God with the power of light and death could summon this much destruction, and he was just that being.

Tears came to his eyes as he observed the void where his city used to be, but found within it a strange moving substance. The true form of Hades walked on his unstable black river, and he was making his way toward the Pyramid.

His ominous presence came to stand before the void, gazing at him with eyes of fire. And when he breathed out his frigid breath, he bowed his head in reverence.

"All souls shall pass," he whispered his deep, sinister prayer.

Derrick watched as he willingly threw himself into the black hole, and then ultimately disappeared. Then in one sweeping motion of his arm, directed the destruction downward, unknowing of where it would go.

The sea and the sky fell. Visions of heaven and all its inhabitants spiraled past him, creating an electrifying storm as it meshed together and then finally disappeared, leaving nothing but a black canvas.

Everything he ever knew and loved in his life was gone, and he would now join with everlasting darkness. The last thought he had was of Katherine and her beauty. Unsure if he'd ever be able to think of her again, he cherished his last vision, burying it deep inside his soul. And just before he disappeared, he saw himself with her once more, telling her of the love he carried for her. And their love, no matter darkness or of light, would ever die.

Chapter Twenty

Light flooded Katherine's senses when she opened her eyes. And the soft sensation on her skin wasn't his fingers, but was the gentle warm breeze off the ocean.

She found herself lying down on the beach in the spot it all started, but this time the sky was crisp blue. The ocean was calm, and the gulls called out a sad song as if knowing what was in her heart.

She breathed a heavy sighed when she sat up in the sand. She pulled her knees to her chest, tears rolling down her cheeks as she gazed at this paradise. It was beautiful and serene, but failed in comparison to Atlantis and to the man she loved more than anything else in the world—or any world for that matter.

"Katherine," a familiar voice spoke from behind her and she recognized it right away. With a quick twist, she rose to her feet and turned to face him, the man she finally knew as her father.

"Ah, my dear," Ian said as he welcomed her into his arms. "You did very well in your task."

She buried her face in his chest and cried. "He's gone."

"He did what was right for our people," he said in reassurance. "Their souls were finally released from a terrible burden because of his sacrifice."

She raised her hopeful eyes to his. "Is he …?"

Ian sighed. "I'm sorry."

Tears welled in her eyes and she found herself back in his comforting arms. He held her for a long moment before he gently pushed her back, gathering her attention on him.

"I have to leave now. I must join your mother and the other survivors in the sea."

"There are survivors in the sea?" she asked, terribly confused as she turned and looked out onto the calm blue waves.

"When Derrick discovered his destiny, he became the universe for one brief moment and all the time rifts were filled in. And since Atlantis sat inside one of those fragments, everything fell away. Some things were lost, but our city and its immortals somehow found the depths of the ocean."

"What will happen now?" she asked in frustration.

"You have a choice, Katherine," he said as he moved between her and the water. "You can come with us to live in the new Atlantis. There are many of us now amongst our city in the sea."

"And what is the other choice?"

"You can stay here and live your life. But if you choose to do this, you will never see us again. You'll never be able to visit, and in time, you'll come to forget everything that has happened and everyone you have met ... including Derrick."

Katherine gripped the gem tight in her hand. No. He was wrong. She could never forget the sacrifice Derrick made, and the love they shared would be forever embedded in her heart.

"I'm so glad to have met you ... Father," she said as she took him by the hand. "I will never forget you."

He sighed. "Are you sure you don't need more time to think about this?"

She shook her head. "No. This place is my home."

With tears glittering in his eyes, he gazed down at her. In a loving manner, he pressed his lips to her forehead and then hugged her tight.

"Then I shall miss you."

"I'll miss you too," she whispered, as he pulled from their embrace and walked out into the sea.

"Oh, by the way," he said turning around. "Everything I have is yours. I've transferred the title into your name along with all my accounts. You'll find all the paperwork inside the drawer near the kitchen. All I ask is for you to stay here for a few weeks before making your way back to London. Recuperate. Give your heart time to heal before you go on with your life."

Seeing her nod, he gave her one last smiling glance and then dove into the waves. She watched him swim out, and then wave as he jumped into the air, showing off his blue fins before he disappeared into the depths forever—going home.

Katherine solemnly smiled as she stepped up the back stairs to the house. The thought of her parents living deep in the ocean somewhere was astounding, and quite complicated to believe, but she did.

Exhaustion set in as she stepped through the sliding glass door and into the quiet house. Loneliness followed her, and tears began to well at the sight of Ian's picture on the wall.

A lasting memory, she thought as she traced his image with her fingers.

She came to the large round mirror in the bedroom and stopped. For a moment, she wasn't sure who stared back at her. But she was sure it wasn't her reflection, for she'd never looked this pitiful before.

She pulled out a yellow sundress and thought of the tub in Derrick's house. What she'd give to be there now, taking in the sweet scent and feeling the bubbles caressing her skin with him by her side.

She stepped into the shower and cried, wishing she could go back to the time in the temple. To touch him again, to feel his arms around her as they made love, would make her feel again, but he was gone, and it hurt in a terrible way to think of him.

She left the shower and tread lightly to the bedroom. Tears fell to the floor with every step she took until she reached the bed. And giving in to exhaustion, she fell into the covers, gripped the gem tight in her hand, and cried herself to sleep.

•

The evening shadows stretched through the room when she opened her eyes. At first she lay there wondering what in the world she'd heard. A seagull screeching outside? Possibly, but whatever the sound, it was loud enough to wake her from much needed sleep.

She'd been back more than a few weeks, but still couldn't find the courage to face the world. Maybe she was afraid to find out what time she'd found herself in, keeping her from contacting anyone. But she knew the real reason why she hadn't left Bimini. It was for fear she'd stop thinking about her time in Atlantis, and most of all the fear of forgetting Derrick.

The sound came again, forcing her eyes wide open. It wasn't a seagull crying outside, or a fog horn blowing in the distant. No, this was the doorbell on her house.

"Go away," she whispered and clutched her pillow close. She wasn't in the mood for visitors, and was sure she'd never want to see anyone again. But she rose from the bed and slipped on her dress.

Immediately shielding her vision with her hand, she found a man walking up the sidewalk toward one of the island jeeps. "Can I help you?" she asked, gathering his attention with her groggy voice.

He turned around and grinned. "I didn't think anyone was home."

"I was sleeping," she retorted, feeling a bit leery as he made his way back toward her.

"I'm sorry," he apologized. "But I've come all this way to meet Ian."

He came to stand right in front of her, but the blasted sun was making it difficult to see him. And with his sunglasses on, she couldn't get a good look at his face.

"Ian's not here," she said as she stepped back through the doorway and began to shut the door, but the stranger's hand stopped her from closing it on him.

"Wait," he said in a serious voice. "He said he had an item for me. One I might be interested in studying."

She looked him over again, but this time with intent to see. The sun was almost set and the figure of the man was becoming clear. His tall frame, muscular and perfect, stood beautifully in a tight fitting white T-shirt. The black slacks he wore matched his expensive dress shoes. And his hair was short, perfectly layered as it slightly curled down around the back of his ears.

Her heart pounded in her chest. If only he'd remove the sunglasses, she could see his eyes, his beautiful sea-green eyes she loved more than anything.

"Are you okay, Miss?" he asked.

Catching herself staring, she quickly turned her attention to the floor as tears formed in her eyes. Though this man had similar features, she knew it wasn't him. Derrick was gone, and she had to find a way to accept it.

"Listen," he said, becoming slightly frustrated with her. "I'm sorry I've put you out, but I really need to talk with Ian. He told me it was very important to come here as soon as possible, that it would be worth my while. I dropped all my projects to be here. So if you don't mind fetching him for me."

"He's not here," she said in a raised voice.

Her angering eyes found their way back to him. The sun had finally set, giving her a better vision. And when he reached up and removed his sunglasses, she immediately lost her breath.

"Derrick?"

His turquoise eyes sparkled in confusion as she covered her mouth with her hand. In overwhelming excitement, she leapt up into his arms and held him tight around his neck, swearing under her breath he was real and not a dream.

"I thought I'd never see you again!" she eagerly cried.

"Hey," he said in a soothing, yet stern voice as he took her by the arms and gently pushed her away. He arched his brow and gave her a peculiar look. "Do we know each other?"

She choked back appalled tears. "Don't you remember me?" She pulled him inside the house.

"I've never met you before in my life," he said stubbornly, stopping abruptly when she closed the door behind them. His worried look suddenly relaxed. "Ah, Ian told you about me then. Though you are a bit unorthodox with your greeting, I'm pleased to meet you. Derrick Sudey. I'm the archaeologist he called a few weeks ago." He took control of his stance and found his business guise. "He told me about an artifact he'd found off the coast here in Bimini and it would be the find of the century ... for my eyes only," he added rather cockily. "So I'm guessing you're either his assistant, or a relative."

Katherine sat down at the kitchen table, completely astounded, appalled, and just downright in shock. Swallowing down apprehension, she tried to fathom the idea he didn't know her—or himself for that matter.

"I'm his daughter," she managed to say.

"I figured as much," he said with a reassured nod. "So, where is this artifact he wanted to show me?"

"I don't know," she answered in a daze.

"Then where is Ian?"

"He's not here."

He stuffed his sunglasses inside his shirt pocket and sighed as he turned to leave. "Well then, this was a waste of my time, but I thank you for yours I suppose."

She watched him walk toward the front door, desperately wanting to stop him, but she was speechless. And too stunned to move, she let him leave without another word.

What was happening here? Had she found herself in another dimension where mermaids live in the ocean, and now former Greek gods roam the earth unknowing of who they are? And why was she letting him leave when he meant everything to her, regardless of what existence she'd ended up in?

On this thought, she fled to the door and swung it open just in time to watch him drive away. With a quick step she ran up the sidewalk and onto the road, yelling for him to stop, but it was too late.

She sprinted up the middle of the dark road, barefoot and frustrated. She ran, trying desperately not to break down. She veered off the road into a small group of trees. And with a careful step, trudged through a small marsh until she reached the helicopter pad where a black chopper was just winding up.

Completely out of breath, she ran underneath the swirling propellers and peered into the pilot side window. It was him, and a sudden breath of enlightenment hit her. She knocked on the window, gathering his attention. But he refused to shut down the engine, even after she opened the door.

"What are you doing?" he yelled angrily as he took hold of the handle, preparing to close the door on her.

"You can't leave!" she yelled over the whir. "Please, shut it down!"

He shook his head. "I have to get back tonight! There's an important meeting in the morning that I can't miss."

"No!" she cried loudly, holding the door rigid so he couldn't close it.

"Let go!" he yelled as he pulled.

His grip was strong, and it was becoming ever difficult to keep the door open. And with the strong winds causing her hair to whip around her face and eyes, she could barely hold on much longer. She had to think of something to say, something to do to keep him here with her.

A strange tingle came from her hand, one much different than the vibration of the chopper. She could see a faint glow working where the gem still held fast on her palm, and then it suddenly dawned on her.

As if the warm gushing wind was telling her what she needed to do, she closed her eyes and listened. The diamond carried his heart, and he'd given it to her on his last words. But now it was time to give him hers, and hope he'd remember.

She opened her eyes and held out her hand. "I think this is what Ian wanted me to give you!" she yelled, feeling the moment thicken as he held out his hand.

"I really need to go," he said as she dropped it perfectly onto his palm.

Katherine nodded and then released the door. In a surreal moment, she stepped back and watched as the helicopter slightly lifted into the sky. But as she began her lonely walk back to the house, it returned to the ground.

She turned to find him standing outside the chopper, hand clutched into a fist. And when she saw him looking at her with his beautiful sea-green eyes, she knew he'd remembered.

She spared no time in leaping into his welcoming arms, and he twirled her around until her feet became solid in the sand. He leaned down and kissed her lips, sending her fearful tears into joyful cries of happiness. And when he parted from her mouth, he opened his hand to show her the diamond.

"I'm so sorry," he said as he clutched the gem tight. "For ten years I've wondered who I am, but I should have remembered you."

She shook her head. "All that matters is you found your way back to me."

He closed his eyes, remembering. "I destroyed everything," he whispered. "My city, the forest—the sea, all of it disappeared into a darkness I created." He cried angrily and fell to his knees. Holding tight to her waist, he pressed his face against her abdomen finding comfort.

She held his head in her hands and stroked his soft hair wanting to take away his pain. The agony he was in was too much to bear, but she would make sure he wouldn't go through it alone.

"What ever terrible things you've endured," she said in a soothing voice. "Just know you're here now, and you're safe with me. I will never leave your side, and you will never leave mine again."

He lifted his head from her comforting hands and gazed up at her. With gentle persuasion, he pulled her down to her knees and inspected her.

"I feel it's been an eternity since I said goodbye to you," he said as he stroked her hair back from her face. "It's strange. I sacrificed my immortal soul for my people, never expecting to be anywhere else but with eternal darkness, but I ended up here somehow."

He grasped her face in his hands and breathed an elusive sigh. "I was found broken as if my body had fallen from the sky to solid ground. I slept for five years in a hospital vividly dreaming about a radiant light—an angel with dark silk hair and lips of red wine." He slid his thumbs softly across her lips. "I could almost touch her, but I could never see her clearly enough to find my way to her side. And when I awoke, I remembered nothing of myself or how I came to be.

"I took the vision of her with me as I made a life for myself in this world, believing one day I would discover her and wake my memory." He intensely gazed into her eyes. "And I swore I would take this beautiful woman who called me from my darkness into my arms and whisper in her ear how much I love her."

"And did you find her?"

He pulled her against him and slid his hands through her hair. As he held her dark strands back away from her face, he pressed his lips to her ear and breathed.

"I would fall through darkness again to be near you," he whispered, making her body tremble. He let go of her hair, grasped the back of her head and kissed her lips. "I would steal the stars from the night sky and lay them at your feet, but they would only bow to your radiance, for you are the angel I have dreamt of, and the woman I love more than all things. You are the goddess of my heart."

He reached into his pocket and then took her by the hand. He placed in her palm a gem, but it wasn't the diamond holding their intertwined hearts. This one was made clear and perfectly set in a golden ring.

"I know the ways of this world now," he said as he gazed into her eyes. "I have a mortal body with a mortal soul. And my heart returned to me when you gave me the diamond, but now I am giving it back to you through this new ring. And if you will have me, I will love you until the end of time."

She cried. And as she met him in a passionate kiss, she knew their hearts would be ultimately sealed in an everlasting embrace. And no darkness, neither in the heavens or the earth, would ever be able to touch their souls again.

•••

Angela Steed

Born in Seattle, Washington, the author grew up
in a small town on the Oregon Coast. After living
in Portland, Oregon, she moved to the beautiful
Appalachian Mountains of West Virginia where she
lives with her husband and two daughters. In addition
to being a novelist, Angela is a licensed realtor, freelance
writer and computer specialist.

www.AngelaSteed.com

Milo March is a hard-drinking, womanizing, wisecracking, James-Bondian character. He always comes out on top through a combination of personality, bluff, bravado, luck, skill, experience, and intellect. He is a shrewd judge of human character, a crack shot, and a deeper character than I have found in most of the other spy/thriller novels I've read. But, above all, he is a con-man—and a very good one. It is Milo March himself who makes the series worth reading.

—Don Miller, *The Mystery Nook* fanzine 12

Steeger Books is proud to reissue twenty-three vintage novels and stories by M.E. Chaber, whose Milo March Mysteries deliver mile-a-minute action and breezily readable entertainment for thriller buffs.

Milo is an Insurance Investigator who takes on the tough cases. Organized crime, grand theft, arson, suspicious disappearances, murders, and millions and millions of dollars—whatever it is, Milo is just the man for the job. Or even the only man for it.

During World War II, Milo was assigned to the OSS and later the CIA. Now in the Army Reserves, with the rank of Major, he is recalled for special jobs behind the Iron Curtain. As an agent, he chops necks, trusses men like chickens to steal their uniforms, shoots point blank at secret police—yet shows compassion to an agent from the other side.

Whatever Milo does, he knows how to do it right. When the work is completed, he returns to his favorite things: women, booze, and good food, more or less in that order....

THE MILO MARCH MYSTERIES

Hangman's Harvest

No Grave for March

The Man Inside

As Old as Cain

The Splintered Man

A Lonely Walk

The Gallows Garden

A Hearse of Another Color

So Dead the Rose

Jade for a Lady

Softly in the Night

Uneasy Lies the Dead

Six Who Ran

Wanted: Dead Men

The Day It Rained Diamonds

A Man in the Middle

Wild Midnight Falls

The Flaming Man

Green Grow the Graves

The Bonded Dead

Born to Be Hanged

Death to the Brides

The Twisted Trap: Six Milo March Stories

Angela Steed

1080 Kiss

"1080 Kiss is anything but chilly!"
Coffee Time Romance

The "God of Snow" has met his match.

Professional snowboarder Vince Evans, "The God of Snow," has met his match in public relations extraordinaire Morgan Price. But will she break the rules of business for this black haired, green eyed bad-boy-turned-good?